BY
TARA PAMMI

All Rights Reserved including the right of reproduction in whole or in part in any form. This edition is published by arrangement with Harlequin Enterprises II B.V./S.à.r.l. The text of this publication or any part thereof may not be reproduced or transmitted in any form or by any means, electronic or mechanical, including photocopying, recording, storage in an information retrieval system, or otherwise, without the written permission of the publisher.

First published in Great Britain 2014
by Mills & Boon, an imprint of Harlequin (UK) Limited,
Eton House, 18-24 Paradise Road, Richmond, Surrey TW9 1SR

© Tara Pammi 2014

First published in Great Britain 2013
by Mills & Boon, an imprint of Harlequin (UK) Limited.
Harlequin (UK) Limited, Eton House, 18-24 Paradise Road,
Richmond, Surrey TW9 1SR

© Tara Pammi 2013

ISBN: 978 0 263 90063 7

Harlequin (UK) policy is to use papers that are natural, renewable and recyclable products and made from wood grown in sustainable forests. The logging and manufacturing process conform to the legal environmental regulations of the country of origin.

Printed and bound in Spain
by Blackprint CPI, Barcelona

Tara Pammi can't remember a moment when she wasn't lost in a book—especially a Mills & Boon® romance, which provided so much more excitement to a teenager than a mathematics textbook. It was only years later, while struggling with her two-hundred-page thesis in a basement lab, that Tara realised what she really wanted to do: write a romance novel. She already had the requirements—a wild imagination and a love for the written word.

Tara lives in Colorado, with the most co-operative man on the planet and two daughters. Her husband and daughters are the only things that stand between Tara and a full-blown hermit life with only books for company.

Tara would love to hear from readers. She can be reached at tara.pammi@gmail.com or at her website: www.tarapammi.com

Recent titles by the same author:

A HINT OF SCANDAL
  (The Sensational Stanton Sisters)

Did you know these are also available as eBooks?

To the man who started it all—my father—
for giving me my love of books, for never holding me
back, for always believing that there was
nothing I couldn't do if I set my mind to it.

CHAPTER ONE

KIMBERLY STANTON STARED at the white rectangle of plastic on the gleaming marble counter in the ladies' bathroom. Terror coated her throat as though it might come to life and take a bite out of her. It looked alien, out of place amidst the lavender potpourri, the crystal lamp settings and the glossy chrome fixtures.

The few minutes stretched like an eternity. The quiet lull of voices outside was exaggerated into distorted echoes.

Her heart beat faster and louder. A painful tug in her lower belly stole her breath. She clutched the cold granite vanity unit and clenched the muscles in her legs, willing herself to hold on.

The scariest word she had ever encountered appeared on the stick.

Pregnant.

No confusing colors or symbols that meant you had to peek again at the box discarded in terrified panic.

Simple, plain English.

Her heart leaped into her throat. Her legs shaking beneath her, she leaned against one of the stalls behind her, dipped her head low and forced herself to breathe past the deafening whoosh in her ears.

Her one mistake, which technically she had committed twice, couldn't haunt her for the rest of her life, could it?

But she couldn't change the consequences. She had never been naïve or stupid enough to wish it either.

She flicked the gleaming chrome tap open and dangled her fingers under the ice-cold water. The sound of the water hitting the sink drowned out the sound of her heartbeat, helping her focus on her breathing.

In, out. In, out...

She closed the tap. Straightening up, she was about to reach for the hand towel when she looked at the mirror and froze.

She stared at her reflection, noting the dark circles under her eyes, the lack of color in her face, the skin pulled tautly over her bones. Drops of water seeped through the thin silk of her blouse to her skin beneath.

She looked as if she was on the brink of a nervous breakdown. And maybe she was. But she didn't have time now. The breakdown had to wait. She touched the tips of her fingers to her temple and pressed. The cold from her almost numb fingers seeped into her overheated skin.

She had no time to deal with this now. She had to compartmentalize—set it aside until she was alone, until she was equipped to think logically, until the shock making her jittery all over faded into nothing more than a numbing ache.

And when it did she would assess the situation again with a clear head, take the necessary action to equip herself better to handle it. It wasn't as if she didn't have any experience with dealing with shock and pain.

Although why she had chosen this particular moment to take the test when the pregnancy kit had been burning a rectangular hole in her handbag for more than a week was anybody's guess. Or maybe she was having another momentary collapse of her rational thinking circuits.

She had been having those moments a lot lately.

She pulled her lip-gloss out of her clutch and reapplied

it with shaking fingers. She ran a hand over her suit. The silky material under her fingers rooted her back to reality.

She needed to get back out there. She needed to circulate among the guests—a specially put together group of investors she had researched for more than six months. Investors who had shown interest in her web startup *The Daily Help*.

She had a presentation to give. She had to talk them through the financial outline she had sketched for the next five years. She had to convince them to invest in *her* startup when there were a million others mushrooming every day.

She had to convince them that the recent scandal about her, Olivia and Alexander had nothing to do with the way she did business. It was a sign of how strong her business proposal was that they had even showed up, despite the scandal.

She straightened her jacket and turned toward the exit. And paused midstride.

Turning back, she picked up the plastic tube, wrapped it carefully in the wrapper she had left on the sink and threw it into the trash. She fumbled when she turned the corner, struggling to breathe past the tight ache in her gut. She placed her hand on her stomach and drew in gulps of air, waiting for the tidal wave of pain that threatened to pull her under to pass.

Striding out of the restroom, she plucked a glass of sparkling water from a passing waiter and nodded at an old friend from Harvard. She was glad she had booked this conference hall in one of the glitzy hotels in Manhattan, even though her tightfisted CFO had frowned over the expense.

Kim didn't think an evening in her company's premises—a large open space in the basement of a building in Manhattan, unstructured in every way possible—would encourage confidence on the investors' part.

She checked her Patek Philipe watch, a gift from her

father when she had graduated from Harvard, and invited everyone to join her in the conference room for the presentation.

She felt an uncharacteristic reluctance as she switched on the projector. Once she concluded the presentation she was going to be alone with her thoughts. Alone with things she couldn't postpone thinking about anymore.

It happened as she reached almost the end of her presentation.

With her laser pointer pointed at a far-off wall, instead of at her company's financial forecast on the rolled-out projector screen, she lost her train of thought—as though someone had turned off a switch in her brain.

She searched the audience for what had thrown her.

A movement—the turn of a dark head—a whisper or something else? Had she imagined it? Everything and everyone else faded into background for a few disconcerting moments. Had her equilibrium been threatened so much by her earlier discovery?

The resounding quiet tumbled her out of her brain fog. She cleared her throat, took a sip of her water and turned back to the chart on the screen. She finished the presentation, her stomach still unsettled.

The lights came on and she smiled with relief. Several hands came up as she opened the floor to questions. She could recite those figures half-asleep. Every little detail of her company was etched into her brain.

The first few were questions she had expected. Hitting her stride, she elaborated on what put her company a cut above the others, provided more details, more figures, increasing statistics and the ad revenue they had generated last year.

Even the momentary aberration of a few minutes ago couldn't mar the satisfaction she could feel running in her veins, the high of accomplishment, of her hard work bearing fruit.

She answered the last question, turned the screen off and switched on the overhead lights.

There *he* was. The reason for the strange tightening in her stomach. The cause of the prickling sensation she couldn't shed.

Diego Pereira. The man who had seduced her and walked away without a backward glance. The man whose baby she was pregnant with.

She froze on the slightly elevated podium, felt her gut falling through an endless abyss. Like the time her twin sister had dragged her on a free-fall ride in an amusement park. Except through the nauseating terror that day she had known that at some point the fall would end. So she had forced herself to sit rigid, her teeth digging painfully into the inside of her mouth, while Liv had screamed with terror and laughter.

No such assurance today. Because every time Diego stormed into her life she forgot the lesson she had learned long ago.

Her hands instinctively moved to her stomach and his gaze zeroed in on her amidst the crowd. She couldn't look at him. Couldn't look into those golden eyes that had set her up to fall. Couldn't look at that cruel face that had purposely played with her life.

She forced herself to keep her gaze straight, focused on all the other curious faces waiting to speak to her. It was the most excruciating half hour of her entire life. She could feel Diego's gaze on her back, drilling into her, looking for a weak spot—anything that he could use to cause more destruction.

At least he'd made it easy for her to avoid him, sitting in one of the chairs in the back row with his gaze focused on her.

She slipped, the heel of one of her three-inch pumps snagging on the carpet as she moved past him. Just the dark scent of him was tripping her nerves.

Why was he here? And what cruel twist of fate had brought him here the very same day she had discovered that she was pregnant?

Diego Pereira watched unmoving as Kim closed the door to the conference hall behind her, her slender body stiff with tension. She was nervous and, devil that he was, he liked it.

He flicked through the business proposal. Every little detail of her presentation was blazing in his mind, and he was impressed despite his black mood. Although he shouldn't really be surprised.

Her pitch for investment today had been specific, innovative, nothing short of exceptional. Like her company. In three years she had taken the very simple idea of an advice column into an exclusive, information-filled web portal with more than a million members and a million more waiting on shortlists for membership.

He closed his eyes and immediately the image of her assaulted him.

Dressed formally, in black trousers that showed off her long legs and a white top that hugged her upper body, she was professionalism come to life—as far as possible from the woman who had cried her pleasure in his arms just a month ago.

He had even forgotten the reason he had come to New York while he had followed her crisp, confident presentation. But the moment she had realized he was present in the audience had been his prize.

She had faltered, searched the audience. That seconds-long flicker in her focus was like a nervous scream for an average woman.

But then there was nothing average about the woman

he had married. She was beautiful, brilliant, sophisticated. She was perfection personified—and she had as much feeling as a lump of rock.

A rock he was finally through with—ready to kick out of his life. It was time to move on, and her little nervous sputter at the sight of him had gone a long way toward pacifying his bitter resentment.

He walked to an elevator and pressed the number for the tenth floor. When he reached her suite he pulled the gold-plated keycard he had bribed from the bellboy from his coat packet.

He entered the suite and closed the door behind him.

The subtle scent of lily of the valley assailed him instantly. It rocked him where he stood, dispensing a swift punch to his gut more lethal than the ones he had taken for half his life.

His lungs expanded, drawing the scent of her deep into him until it sank once again into his blood.

His body pulsed with remembered pleasure. Like a junkie getting his high.

He studied the suite, with its luxurious sitting area and mahogany desk. Her files were neatly stacked on it, her sleek state-of-the-art laptop on top of them. Her handbag—a practical but designer black leather affair—lay near the couch in the sitting area.

The suite was everything its owner was—high-class, flawless and without an ounce of warmth.

He turned at the sound of a door on his right.

Closing the door behind her, she leaned against it. A sheen of sweat danced on her forehead.

He frowned, his curiosity spiking.

Her glistening mouth trembled as she spotted him, her hands moving to her midriff.

There was a distinct lack of color to her skin. Her slender shoulders quivered as she ran the back of her hand over her forehead.

He looked at her with increasing curiosity. Her jacket was gone. A V-necked sleeveless white silk blouse showed off her toned arms. The big steel dial of her designer watch highlighted her delicate wrist. A thin gold chain dangled at her throat.

The shadow of her breasts beneath the thin silk drew his gaze.

He swallowed and pulled his eyes up. The memory of her breasts in his hands was cutting off his breath more effectively than a hand choking his windpipe. The feel of her trembling with pleasure in his hands, the erotic scent of her skin and sex—images and sensations flooded through him.

He could no more fight the assault than he could stop breathing.

Her eyes flared wide, the same heat dancing in those chocolate depths.

She was the very embodiment of perfection—always impeccably dressed, exuding the sophistication that was like a second skin to her. Yet now she looked off-balance.

He reached her, the slight sway of her lithe figure propelling him toward her. "Are you okay, *gatinha?*"

She ran her palm over her face, leaving pink fingerprints over her colorless skin. Stepping away from him, she straightened the already immaculate desk. Her fingers trembled as she picked up a pen and moved it to the side.

She was more than nervous.

"No, I'm not," she said, shrugging those elegant shoulders. The frank admission was unusual. "But that's not a surprise as I just saw *you,* is it?"

He raised a brow and sliced the distance between them. "The sight of me makes you sick?"

Her fingers clutched the edge of the desk, her knuckles

white. "The sight of you reminds me of reckless stupid behavior that I'd rather not remember."

He smiled. "Not even the good parts, where you screamed?"

Pink scoured her cheeks. The slender set of her shoulders straightened in defense. She moved to the sitting area and settled into a leather chair. "Why are you here, Diego?"

He watched with a weird fascination as she crossed her legs and looked up at him.

The nervousness he had spied just moments ago had disappeared. She sounded steady, without a hint of anger or upset. Even though the last time they had laid eyes on each other she had been half-naked in his bed, her face bereft of color as he had dressed and informed her that he was done with her.

There was no reproach in her tone for *his* behavior a month ago.

Her calm composure grated on him like the edge of a saw chipping away at wood.

She drove him to be the very worst of himself—seething with frustration, thrumming with desire—whereas she remained utterly unaffected.

He settled down on the coffee table in front of her and stretched his legs so that she was trapped between them. He flipped open the file next to him against his better instincts, to finish what he had come for. "Your proposal is brilliant."

"I don't need you to tell me that," she threw back, her chin jutting out.

He smiled. The confidence creeping back into her tone was not a surprise. When it came to her company his estranged wife was a force to be reckoned with. "Is that your standard response to a potential investor?"

She snorted, and even that was an elegant movement of her straight nose. "It's my standard response to a man who I know is intent on causing me maximum damage."

Diego frowned. "Really? Have I done that?"

She snatched the proposal from his hands and the scent of her wafted over him. He took a breath and held it fast, the muscles in his abdomen tightening.

Droga, two minutes in her company and he was...

He expelled it with the force of his self-disgust. Pleasure was *not* the reminder he needed.

"You already had your revenge, Diego. After I walked out on our marriage six years ago you refused to divorce me with the express purpose of ruining my wedding to Alexander. Then you seduced me and walked out four weeks ago. Isn't that enough?"

"Seeing that you went back to your life, didn't even falter for a second, I'm not sure."

Something flickered in her molten brown gaze as she spoke. "I propelled my sister and Alex into a scandal, putting everything Alex has worked for at risk."

"Again, *them*—not you. From where I stand nothing has gotten to you. Apparently nothing *ever* gets to you."

She ran her fingers over her nape, her gaze shying away from him. Sudden tension pulsed around her. "You left me utterly humiliated and feeling like a complete fool that morning. Is that better?"

He had wanted her anger, her pain, and it was there in her voice now, thrumming with force. But it was too little, too late. Even now it was only the prospect of her precious company having caught his interest that was forcing any emotion from her.

"Maybe," he said, shrugging off his jacket.

Her gaze flew to his, anxious. "Tell me—what do I need to say so that you'll leave my company alone? What will save it from the utter ruin you're planning?"

"I thought your confidence in your company was unshakeable? Your strategy without pitfalls?"

"Not if you make it your life's mission to destroy it," she

said. Her voice rang with accusation, anger, and beneath it all, a curious hurt. "That's what this is all about, isn't it? Anyone who crosses you, who disappoints you, you ensure their ruin. Now it's my turn."

She straightened, her hands folded at her middle. The action pushed her small breasts into prominence. He trained his gaze on her face as though his life depended on it. Maybe not his life, but his very sanity relied on his self-control.

He didn't plan to lose it again.

"Six years ago you were obsessed with revenge, driven by only one goal—to ruin your father. You didn't care who you hurt in the process. You took his small construction company and expanded it into an empire—encompassing energy generation, mining. If I were to believe the media—and knowing you personally I'm very much inclined to—you are called a bastard with alarming frequency. You crushed anything that got in your way. Including your own father." She shot up from the seat and paced the length of the room. "I don't believe in wasting precious time fighting the inevitable. So whatever you're about to do—do it. But I won't go down without a fight. My company—"

"Means everything to you, right? You should be held up as an example to anyone who doubts that women can be as unfeeling and ruthless as men," he interjected smoothly, feeling that flare of anger again.

She stared at him, her gaze puzzled. "Why do I get the feeling that that's not a compliment?"

"It's not."

Her fingers tightened on the windowsill behind her. "We're even now, Diego. Let's just leave it at that."

He moved closer. He could see his reflection in her eyes, her slender shoulders falling and rising with her rapid breathing. Her gaze moved to his mouth and he felt a roar of desire pummel through his blood. It was impossible not to remember how good she had felt, how she had wrapped her legs around him and urged him on with soft little growls.

If he kissed her she wouldn't push him away. If he ran the pad of his thumb over the pulse beating frantically at her throat she wouldn't argue. She would be putty in his hands.

Wasn't that why he felt such a physical pull toward her? Because when he touched her, when he kissed her, it was the one time he felt that he owned this woman—all of her. Her thoughts, her emotions, the core of her.

He fisted his hands. But it would prove nothing new—to him or to her. Self-disgust boiled through him for even thinking it. He had let her get to him on the island, burrow under his skin until the past six years had fallen away and he'd been standing there with her letter in hand.

Never again.

He needed a new beginning without being haunted by memories of this woman. He needed to do what he had come for and leave—*now.*

"I realized what I had done wrong the moment I left the island," he said, unable to stop himself from wringing out the last drop of satisfaction. He had never claimed to be a great man. He had been born a bastard, and to this day he *was* one. "I've come to rectify that mistake."

Kim trembled all over, an almighty buzz filling up her ears.

"A mistake?" Her throat ached as it pushed that word out.

His golden gaze gleamed, a knowing smile curving his upper lip. "I forgot a tiny detail, although it was the most important of all."

He plucked a sheaf of papers from his coat pocket and slid them on to her desk. Every inch of her tensed. The words on those familiar papers blurred.

"I need your signature on the divorce papers."

She struggled to get her synapses to fire again, to get her lungs to breathe again.

The innocuous-looking papers pierced through her defenses, inviting pain she had long ago learned not to feel. This was what she had wanted for six long years—to be able to correct the mistake she had made, to be able to forget the foolish dream that had never stood a chance.

Her palms were clammy as she picked up the papers.

"My staff at the villa were never able to locate the copies you brought."

She shivered uncontrollably at the slight curiosity in his words. *Because she had torn them up after that first night when Diego had made love to her.*

No, not *love*. Sex. Revenge sex. The this-is-what-you-walked-away-from kind. For a woman with an above average IQ, she had repeated the same mistake when it came to Diego.

She turned the papers over and over in her hands. *This was it.*

Diego would walk out of her life. She would never again have to see the foolishness she had indulged in in the name of love. What she had wanted for so long was within her grasp. Yet she couldn't perform the simple task of picking up the pen.

"You could have sent this through your lawyer," she said softly, the shock and confusion she had held in check all evening by the skin of her teeth slithering their way into her. Her stomach heaved. "You didn't have to come yourself."

He leaned against the table, all cool arrogance and casual charm. But nothing could belie the cruel satisfaction in the curve of his mouth. He wanted blood and he was circling her like a hungry shark now that he could smell it.

"And miss the chance to say goodbye for the final time?"

"You mean you wanted to see the fallout from your twisted seduction?"

"Seduction?" he said, a dark shadow falling over his features. The force of his anger slammed into her like a gale.

"Why don't you own it, like you do everything else? There *was* no seduction." He reached her before she could blink. "What does it say about us that even after six years it took us mere hours after laying eyes on each other to end up in bed? Or rather against the wall..."

Her stomach somersaulted. Her skin sizzled. He was right. Sex was all she could think of when he was close. Hot, sweltering, out-of-control, mind-blowing, biggest-mistake-of-your-life-*that-you-made-twice* sex.

She would die before she admitted how much truth there was in his words, how much more he didn't know.

She grabbed her pen and signed the first paper, her fingers shaking.

She lifted her chin and looked up at him, gathering every ugly emotion simmering beneath the surface and pouring it into her words. "It's nothing more than a stimulus and response—like Pavlov's dog. No matter how many years pass, I see you and I think of sex. Maybe because you were my first. Maybe because you are so damn good at it."

The papers slithered to the floor with a dangerous rustle. She felt his fury crackling around them. He tugged her hard against him, his body a smoldering furnace of desire.

She had angered him with her cold analogy. But it only made the void inside her deepen.

His mouth curled into a sneer. "Of course. I forgot that the cruise, those couple of months you spent with me, were nothing but a rich princess's wild, dirty rebellion, weren't they?"

She felt a strange constriction in her chest, a tightness she had nothing to fight against. A sob clawed its way up her throat.

She hated him for ruining the most precious moments of her life. For reducing them to nothing. She hated herself for thinking he had loved her six years ago, for losing her mind the moment she had seen him again four weeks ago.

For someone who had been emotionally stunted for so long, the upsurge of emotion was blinding—pulling her under, driving reason from her mind.

She bunched her fingers in his jacket, his heart thundering beneath her touch. "It's good that you're so greedy you came back for more. Because I have news for you."

CHAPTER TWO

"You have news…?" He frowned, his fingers locked in a tight grip over hers. "What, *princesa?* Do you have a new man lined up now that your sister has stolen the last one? Do you think I give a damn?"

"I'm pregnant."

He didn't move. He didn't blink. Not even a muscle twitched in his mobile face.

Hot satisfaction fueled her. She had wanted to shake his infuriating arrogance. *She had.* On its heels followed raking guilt.

Her knees buckled under her. Only Diego's hold on her was keeping her upright.

God, she hadn't meant to blurt it out like that. She hadn't even dealt with what it meant to *her,* what it implied…

What did it say about her that the only positive thing she felt about the pregnancy was that it could shock Diego like nothing else could?

After the way he had treated her she owed him nothing. And yet keeping him in the dark required a price higher than she was willing to pay.

He had provided her with the best opportunity to tell him, to get it done with. For all she knew he wouldn't even care. He had wanted revenge, he'd got it—with little scruples—and now he had divorce papers ready. And he would keep on walking.

His gaze sliced to her, searching her face. Her composure unraveled at his silence.

The roguish arrogance was gone from his face, replaced by a resolute calm. Every inch of her quaked.

"Is it mine?"

Her gut started that dangerous fall again. She needed to get herself under control. Because Diego was a master at reading her. Whatever she wished, he would do the opposite. Just to make her life harder.

She needed to play it cool. "Why do you think I'm giving *you* the good news?"

"You slept with me mere *hours* after laying eyes on me again," he said, his golden gaze betraying his fury, "while the man you were ready to marry still had his lapdog out looking for you and your twin was being your damned *placeholder* in his life."

She trembled as he walked away from her, as though he couldn't bear to breathe the same air as her.

"And you went back to him as soon as I left you. Except he was two-timing *you* just as you were doing him. So I repeat: is the baby mine?"

"That's not true. Alex and I—"

She shut her mouth with a snap, leaned back against the soft leather, trembling from head to toe. Guilt hung heavy in her stomach. The media, her father—the whole world had crucified Liv, while Kim was the one responsible for it all.

Except Diego knew where she had been and what she had been up to while Liv had pretended to be her. And of course Diego thought Kim had quietly crawled back to Alex, that nothing had changed for her. That she had jumped into his bed from Alex's and then jumped straight back.

That was untrue on so many levels.

Even before Diego had made his true intentions known

Kim had broken it off with Alexander. Only Diego didn't know that.

Her next breath filled her with his scent—dark and powerful. Her eyes flew open.

He raised a brow, watching her with hawklike intensity. "It's a simple question, *gatinha,* and sadly one only a woman can answer."

There was nothing in his tone—no nuance of sarcasm, no hint of anger or accusation—nothing that she could latch onto and feed her fury, her misery.

"Alex and I…" she whispered, feeling heat creep up her skin. "We—"

"All I need—" his words came through gritted teeth "—is your word. Not a day-by-day update on your sexual activity."

Mortification spread like wildfire inside her. Really, she needed to get a grip on herself—needed to stop blurting out things Diego had no need to know.

More information on her non-existent sex-life fell into that category without a doubt. She already had a permanent reminder of how scandalously she had behaved. And now Alex and Liv, her father—*the whole world* was going to find out…

Her gut churned again with a vicious force. "Of course it's yours."

His jaw tight, he nodded. His easy acceptance, his very lack of a reaction, sent a shiver running down her spine. She had expected him to burst out, had braced herself for an attack.

Why did he trust her so easily? He had every right to demand a paternity test. Every right to question the truth of her claim. That was what she wanted from him. That was what she expected from him.

Instead his self-possession—something she usually prided *herself* on—grated on her nerves. She was still panicking. She had blurted out the news in a petty fit of pique. Whereas he didn't even blink.

She laughed, the sound edging toward hysteria. "What? No accusations? No demands for proof? No talk of DNA tests? Just like that, Diego?"

He turned away from her to lean against the wall and closed his eyes. He ran his hand over the bump on his nose. Tension overflowed from him, filling up the huge suite, rattling like an invisible chain, reaching for her. His eyes flew open and her gaze was caught by his.

"DNA tests are for women to whom being pregnant with a rich man's child means a meal ticket to a better life. An accusation my father threw at my mother every time she showed up with me on his doorstep, begging for support."

His words vibrated with emotion. His very stillness, in contrast to the loathing in his words, was disquieting in the least. "However, with our history, I don't think that's what you're going for."

Kim tucked her head in her hands, wondering what she had started. A lump of something—she refused to call it gratitude—blocked her throat, making it harder for her to speak. He could have turned this into something ugly if he wished. *He hadn't.*

Everything within her revolted at being obligated to him for even that small display of honor. It made her weak, plunged her into useless wishing.

She couldn't let him put her in the wrong. She couldn't forget that the very reason she was in this situation was because he had orchestrated payback.

She felt the hard wall of heat from his body and stiffened.

"For a woman who fairly blazes with confidence in every walk of life, your hesitation would be funny if it wasn't the matter of a child. Are you not so sure who the father is yourself?" he whispered softly, something deadly vibrating in his tone.

"There's no doubt," she repeated.

Thinking with a rational mind, she knew she should just tell Diego the stupid truth. That she had never slept with Alexander. But then Diego would never leave the truth alone.

"Now that we have solved that particular puzzle, what do you need from me?"

It took her a moment to realize that he was waiting for an answer. A chill began to spread over her skin. "I...I don't need *anything* from you."

"Of course not." An edge crept into his tone, his gaze devouring her. Something stormy rumbled under that calm now. "Then why tell me?"

"Honestly? I wasn't thinking," she said, wondering if she was destined always to make mistakes when it came to him. "You were gloating. You were..."

"Nice to know something touches you," he said, a fire glinting in his gaze. She opened her mouth to argue and shut it just as quickly. "And if I hadn't been here to gloat? Would you have called me then?"

"That's a question I don't have to answer, because you *are* here. And stop pretending as though this means something, Diego. You were ready to walk out of my life, and I say keep on walking."

"Your arrogance in thinking that you know me is astounding, *querida*. Did I teach you nothing four weeks ago?"

His words rumbled around her, and images and sensations tumbled toward her along with them. But she refused to back down. "You take risks. Your business tactics are barely on this side of the law. The last thing you need in your life is a baby. If I had hidden this from you you would have only found more reason to hate me."

"To think for a moment I assumed that you weren't doing

this for purely selfish reasons but for the actual wellbeing of the child you're carrying…"

She flinched, the worst of her own fears crystallized by his cutting words. Her earlier dread intensified. That was what she should have immediately thought of. *The child's welfare.* "I want nothing but a divorce and an exit from you."

His laughter faded and shadowed intent filled his face. He grabbed the papers she had signed not five minutes ago and shredded them with his hands.

His calm movements twisted her gut. "Then what do you have in mind? We'll kiss each other and make up? Play happy family—"

He came closer—until she could see the gold specks in his eyes, smell the dark scent of him that scrambled her wits.

"I'm not turning my back on my child."

Panic unfurling in her stomach, she shot up from her seat. "You're out of your mind. This is not what I planned for my life—"

"I'm sure you had a list of requirements that needed to be met in order to produce the perfect offspring," he said, his words ringing with bitter satisfaction, "but it's out of your hands now."

"It is. But what I *can* control is what I do about it now. Being a mother is going to be hard enough. Dealing with you on a regular basis will just tip me over into…"

Perverse anger rose within her—perverse, irrational and completely useless. He could walk away from this. She *needed* him to walk away from this. But *she*…she had no such choice. She had a lifelong commitment. She was supposed to love this baby. She was supposed to…

"You don't want this baby?"

"Of course I don't. I'll even go so far as to say it's the

worst thing that has ever happened to me!" she shouted, the words falling off her trembling lips.

Shock flickered in his gaze, but she didn't have the energy to wish them unsaid.

"This baby is going to be a walking, talking reminder of the biggest mistake of my life. You've achieved what you wanted, Diego. You've done your worst. You have changed my life in a way I can't control. Now, please, leave me to get on with it."

Diego breathed out through his teeth and hit the punching bag again with renewed force. His right hook was beginning to fall short again. The injury to the muscle in his bicep was making itself known. The same injury that had forced him to withdraw from financially lucrative streetfights. The injury that had forced him to reach out to his father for help when he had been sixteen and unable to pay for his mother's treatment.

But he wouldn't stop now. He breathed through the vicious pain, hating himself for even remembering.

The clock on the wall behind him chimed, reminding him he'd been at it for more than two hours now.

Sweat poured down from his forehead and he shook his head to clear it off. His T-shirt was drenched through and the muscles in his arms felt like stones. Adrenaline rushed through him in waves and he was beginning to hear a faint thundering in his ears. Probably his blood whooshing. But he didn't stop.

Because even trying to drown himself in physical agony he couldn't block out Kim's words.

Stimulus and response!

Meu Deus, the woman reduced him to the lowest denominator with her infuriating logic. No one had ever got under his skin like she did. And she was carrying his baby.

The resentment that had glittered in her brown eyes pierced even the haze of his pain.

Punch.

Of course it's yours.

Thump.

It's the worst thing that has ever happened to me.

Punch.

This baby is going to be a walking, talking reminder of the biggest mistake of my life.

Thump.

Nausea whirled at the base of his throat, threatening to choke him with its intensity. He'd had enough rejection from his father to last him several lifetimes. He would be dead before he did the same to his child or became a stranger.

He took one last punch and pulled his gloves off. He picked up a bottle of water, guzzled half of it down and dumped the rest over his head. The water trickled over his face into his eyes. The biting cold did nothing to pacify the crazy roar in his head.

Because Kim had been right. He didn't want to be a father.... He wasn't fit to be a father...

He let a curse fly and went at the punching bag again, shame and disgust boiling over in his blood. Pain waves rippled up his knuckles. His skin started peeling at his continued assault.

He had no good in him. All he had was hatred, jealousy. He didn't possess a single redeeming quality that said he should even be a *part* of a child's life. He had chosen to walk the path he had with full clarity of thought—to take everything from his father that he deserved. He had known exactly what he was doing when he'd reached for that goal.

And that was what he wanted to do now, too. He wanted to take his child from Kim and walk away. Every nerve in him wanted to ensure he had full custody.

But he could not sink so low again.

He had let his hatred for his father lead him to destroy his half brother's life in the process. If not for Diego's blind obsession Eduardo would have been...

He shivered, a chill swamping him.

He couldn't risk that happening with his child. If, because of his obsession with Kim, he hurt his child in any way he wouldn't be able to live with himself. He couldn't let his anger at her drive him into making a mistake again— not anymore. Not when it could hurt his own child.

Playing happy family with Kim, seeing her every day, when she was the one weakness he had never conquered— every inch of him revolted at the very thought.

And yet he couldn't escape his responsibility. He couldn't just walk away and become a stranger to his own child.

He had a chance to change the vicious cycle of neglect and abuse he and Eduardo had gone through.

He would move mountains to make sure his child had everything he'd never had—two loving parents and a stable upbringing. Even if that meant tying himself to the woman who brought his bitterest fears to the surface.

CHAPTER THREE

KIM PULLED THE satin pillow over her head and groaned as her cell phone chirped. She hadn't gotten into bed until three in the morning, after going over the new feature on *The Daily Help* with the design architect and writing her own feature for the career advice section she did every Tuesday.

Pushing her hair out of her eyes, she looked at the digital clock on the nightstand. It was only seven. She felt a distinct lack of energy to attack the day. When her phone rang for the third time in a row she switched the Bluetooth on.

"Kim, are you okay?"

Liv.

Tension tightened in the pit of her stomach at the concern in her twin's voice. She had been putting Liv off for two weeks now.

She pushed herself up on the bed and leaned against the metallic headboard. "I'm fine. Is everything okay with you and Alex?"

"We're fine. I'm just…" Liv's uncharacteristic hesitation hung heavily between them. "God, Kim—is it true? Why the hell didn't you *tell* me?"

Kim swallowed, fear fisting her chest. "What are you talking about?"

"You've made front page headlines. Not just the scandal rags, like I did, but even the business channels on television."

"What?"

"It says you're pregnant. Are you?"

Diego.

Kim closed her eyes and breathed huge gulps of air. Obviously her refusal to have anything to do with him, her refusal even to answer his calls, meant Diego had begun playing dirty.

"Yes."

"When were you going to tell me? Are you...? I mean, are you okay with this? Does Diego know? What are you planning to *do?*"

They were all perfectly valid questions. Kim had just shoved them down forcefully.

"I'm perfectly fine, Liv. I don't have the time right now to process what it means. Once this upcoming milestone for my company has passed I'll make a list of the things I need to do." She closed her eyes, fighting for composure. "I'll even have a few sessions with Mommy Mary."

"Who is Mommy Mary?"

"The expert on all things maternal on my team."

"On *what?*"

"On what I need to learn to be the perfect mother. It's not like *we* had a good example, is it?"

"And until then you're just going to put it on the back burner?"

What else was she supposed to do? Focus on the relentlessly clammy feeling in her stomach every time her thoughts turned to the baby growing in her womb?

The stark contrast between the terrifying emptiness *she* felt and her newly pregnant CFO's glorious joy was already a constant distressing reminder that something vital was missing in her own genetic make-up.

"I can't botch this opportunity for my company by losing my focus."

"I don't know what to..." Olivia's tone rang with the

same growing exasperation Kim had sensed in their recent conversations. "Let me know if you need anything, okay?"

Kim tucked her knees close as Liv hung up. She wanted to reach out to Liv. Liv's love came with no conditions, no judgment.

But Kim—she had always been the strong one. She had had to be in order to protect first her mother and then Liv from their father's wrath.

She couldn't confide her fears in anyone. Least of all to her twin, to whom loving and caring and nurturing came so easily.

Whereas Kim had trained herself so hard to not care, not to let herself be touched by emotions. She'd had to after she had learned what her mother had planned...

Only had she accomplished it so well—just as she had everything else in life—that she felt nothing even for the child growing in her womb?

Because even after a week all she felt was utter panic at the thought of the baby. She had spent a fortune buying almost a dozen more pregnancy test kits, hoping that it had been a false positive. And every time the word "pregnant" had appeared her stomach had sunk a little lower.

Or was it because of the man who had fathered her baby? Could her anger for Diego be clouding everything else? Was this how their mother had felt? Beneath her fear of their father, had she felt nothing for her children?

Without crawling out of bed, she pulled her reading glasses on and powered up her iPad. Her heart thumped loudly. She clicked on to one of her favorite websites—one she could count on to provide news objectively.

The Daily Help's pregnant CEO Kimberly Stanton's best kept secret—a secret marriage or the identity of her unborn baby's father?

It was the first time she wasn't in the news being lauded for one of her accomplishments.

The article, for all its flaming header, didn't spend time speculating on the answer to either of the questions it posed. But suddenly she wished it did. Because the speculation it *did* enter into was much more harmful than if they had spawned stuff about her personal life.

The article highlighted the way any woman—especially one who was pregnant and with her personal life in shambles—could expect to expand her company and do it successfully.

Should investors be worried about pouring their money into a company whose CEO's first priority might not be the company itself? One who has been involved in not one but two major scandals? Could this pregnancy herald the death of the innovative startup *The Daily Help* and its brilliant CEO Kimberly Stanton's illustrious career?

She shoved the tablet away and got out of bed, her mind whirling with panic. She ran a hand over her nape, too restless to stay still. It might have been written by Kim herself, for it highlighted every little one of her insecurities—everything she had made a list of herself.

For so long she had poured everything she had into first starting her company and then into making it a financial success. She had never stopped to wonder—never had a moment of doubt when it came to her career.

She opened the calendar on her phone. Her day was full of follow-up meetings with five different investors. By the end of the day she intended to start working on putting the plans she had outlined about the expansion of her company into full gear.

She couldn't focus on any other outcome—couldn't

waste her mental energies speculating and in turn proving the contentious article right.

Only then would she deal with Diego. There was no way anyone else would have known or leaked the news to the media. She had confided in only one person.

Wasn't this what Diego had intended all along? She was a fool if she'd thought even for a moment that he wanted anything but her ruin.

Kim clicked End on her Skype call and leaned back in her chair. Her day had only gotten worse since Liv's phone call. That had been her fifth and last unsuccessful investor meeting. Not one investor was ready to wire in funds.

Whereas the invoices for the new office space she had leased, for the three new state-of-the-art servers she had ordered, for the premium health insurance she had promised her staff this year mocked her and the vast sum of numbers on the papers in front of her was giving her a headache.

She leaned her head back and rubbed the muscles knotting her neck. Her vision for her company, her team's livelihood, both were at stake because she had weakened.

Hadn't she learned more than once how much she could lose if she let herself feel?

The number of things she needed to deal with was piling up. Panic breathed through her, crushing her lungs and making a mockery of the focus that she was so much lauded for. She forced large gulps of air into her lungs.

Breathe in...out...in...out... She repeated it for a few minutes, running her fingers over the award plaques she kept next to her table, searching for something to tune out the panic.

Pull yourself together, Kim. There are people counting on you.

It was the same stern speech she had given herself at thirteen, when she had discovered her mother's packed bag one night. And the note to her father that had knocked the breath from her.

She had survived that night. She could survive anything.

She had to go on as before—for her company's sake and for her own sake. If she lost her company she had nothing. She *was* nothing.

She picked up her cell phone and dialed Alex's number. He was someone with whom she had always tossed around ideas for her business, someone she absolutely trusted. And someone she had been avoiding for the past month…

But she needed objective, unbiased advice, and Alex was the only one who would give it to her. She would exhaust every possibility if it meant she could go on with the plan for expanding her company.

Diego cursed, cold fury singing through his blood as he stared at the live webcast on his tablet. Reporters were camped with cameras and news crews in front of Kim's apartment complex in Manhattan.

He rapped on the partitioning glass and barked her address at his chauffeur.

His gaze turning back to the screen again, he frowned at a sudden roar in the ruckus. And cursed again with no satisfaction as he recognized the tall figure. Her ex had arrived. Diego could almost peek into how the press's mind would work.

The news about her pregnancy on top of the scandal last month, when her twin had been found with Kim's ex—the press would come to only one conclusion.

That the unborn child—his child—was Alexander King's.

This was not what he had intended when he'd had his head of security leak the news of her pregnancy to the media.

He stared at the tall figure of Alexander King as he

walked into the complex without faltering, despite the reporters swarming around him. Acrid jealousy burned through him. He slammed his laptop shut, closed his eyes and sought the image of Eduardo's frail body.

Which was enough to soak up the dark thoughts and send some much-needed reason into his head.

He had done this before—let his obsession consume his sense of right or wrong. He had let it blind him to the fact that Eduardo had needed his help, and instead he'd turned on him.

He couldn't do that again. This was not about what Kim could drive him to. It was about what was right for their child.

Kim took a sip of her water as Alex finished a call. She had emailed him her proposal and set up the appointment. Now she wished she had waited for the weekend. Stupid of her not to expect how much the media would make of Alex visiting her *alone* on a Friday evening at her apartment.

She had never been more ashamed of herself. It had taken everything in her to ask Alex for his help but she had no other options. A flush overtaking her, she plucked up the daily statistics report her website manager had sent her.

Based on the turnover of her company in the last quarter, and on her expansion proposal, investing in her company was a sound opportunity for any shrewd businessman. Except for the scandal she had brought on herself.

Their daily numbers, the number of questions that came into their portal and the website hits, had spiked well above average today.

But she knew, as was pointed out by the breakdown in front of her, that this was because twenty percent of the questions had been about her pregnancy, whether she was married and—worst of them all—whether she was married to the father of her baby.

She needed to make a statement soon.

Tucking his phone into his pocket, Alex turned toward her. "I'm sorry, Kim. You know how much I trust your business savvy. But, as brilliant as your plan and forecast is, I can't invest in it right now."

Her stomach turning, Kim nodded. It was exactly as she had expected: the worst.

She blinked back tears as he wrapped an arm around her. "With everything going on out there right now I just... As much as I hate to admit it, my association with your company in the current climate would only damage your credibility."

Kim nodded, the comfort he offered making her spectacular failure even harder to bear. "I know. And I'm so sorry for putting you and Liv through this—for everything. If I could I would go back to that day and do everything differently." She smiled and corrected herself. "Well, except for the part where I left you with Liv."

He laughed, and her mounting panic was blunted by the sheer joy in that sound. "You don't have to go through this alone, Kim. You should come and stay with—"

"She's not alone to deal with this. And I would think twice, if I were you, before touching my wife again."

Kim jerked around so quickly that her neck muscles groaned.

Diego stood leaning against the door of her apartment, a dark, thundering presence, and he looked at them with such obvious loathing that her mouth dried up.

Next to her, Alex stayed as calm as ever as he turned around. Just like her, he knew who was behind the leak to the media. But, gentleman that he was, he hadn't asked her one personal question.

The very antithesis of the man smoldering with anger at the door.

Mortification heating her cheeks, she met Diego's gaze.

"Don't do this, Diego. Don't make me regret ever knowing you."

He shrugged, the movement stretching the handmade grey silk tight over his muscular frame. "Don't you already? Aren't you going to introduce your husband to your ex, *querida*?"

Alex moved at her side, reaching Diego before she could blink. Her breath hitched in her throat as they both looked at each other.

"Call me anytime, and for any kind of help, Kim," Alex said.

Without another word he strolled out, closing the door behind him. The silence pulling at her stressed nerves, Kim walked past the sitting area to her kitchen, the open layout giving her an unobstructed view of Diego. She pulled a bottle of orange juice out of the refrigerator and poured it into a glass.

Diego leaned against the pillar that cut off the kitchen from the lounge. She raised the glass to her mouth and took a sip. His continued scrutiny prickled her skin. Every time she laid eyes on him she felt as if she was one step closer to a slippery slope.

"What is this? A lesson in caveman behavior?"

"I don't understand your relationship with that man."

She blinked at his soft tone. "Don't turn this around on *me*. Were you going to beat your chest and drag me to your side by my hair if he hadn't left?"

He smiled, his gaze moving to her hair. He flexed his fingers threateningly. "I've never done that before...but if anyone can push me to it, it's you."

Her mouth open, she just stared at him.

"You like throwing my background in my face, don't you? I'm not ashamed that my life began on the streets of Rio de Janeiro, that I used my fists for survival."

She glared at him, insulted by his very suggestion. "It's

got nothing to do with your background and everything to
do with how you are acting now."

"True. This one's my fault. I should have expected you
to go to him for help."

It was the last thing she'd expected him to say.

Calling her a few names, maybe challenging her word
about the paternity of the baby as the whole world was hotly
speculating—sure. But this? No. His continuing trust in her
word threw her, kept her off-balance.

Or was that what he truly intended?

The doubts assailing her, the real possibility of her company falling apart, filled her veins with ice. "As you have
made it your mission to destroy my life, I went crawling
for help to the man whom I deceived dreadfully by sleeping with you. *Satisfied?*"

Diego let his gaze travel lazily over Kim. A long-sleeved
white cotton top hugged her slim torso and the flat of her
stomach, followed by tight blue jeans that encased her long
legs. Her short hair was pulled back with a clip, leaving
shorter tendrils teasing her cheekbones.

He believed her that the baby was his. She had nothing
to gain by lying to him and everything to lose.

Except he didn't understand how, having been almost
literally dragged from the altar by Diego, away from a man
who was now *apparently* happily married to her twin, Kim
could still share a relationship with Alexander that wasn't
the least bit awkward.

Was she still pining after him? After all, she had gone
to him for help. That in itself was revealing.

"I gave you a week, *gatinha*. I refuse to be ignored. I
refuse to let you put your company before the baby and—"

She put her glass down with a force that splashed the
juice onto her fingers. Her posture screamed with barely
contained anxiety. "The baby's not going to be here for

nine months. Do you expect me to sit around twiddling my thumbs until then? I'm not going to give up something I have built with sheer hard work just because I'm pregnant."

There it was again. Her complete refusal to accept that things were going to change.

"I expect you to slow down. I expect you to return my calls. I expect you to stop working sixteen-hour days." She didn't look like perfection put together today. She looked tired and stressed out. Guilt softened his words. "You look like you're ready to fall apart."

"And whose fault is that? I've been trying to minimize the damage you've caused with your dirty tricks."

"You have no idea *how* dirty I'll fight for what I want. Propelling you toward *him* wasn't what I intended, however. But I had forgotten how stubbornly independent you are."

"Careful, Diego. You sound almost jealous. And yet I know you don't give a hoot about me."

"Remember I'm an uncivilized, dirty thug," he said, with a slanted look at her. "A street-fighting Brazilian, *pequena*. Of course I'm jealous."

Kim wiped her fingers on a hand towel, feeling a flush creep up her neck.

Of course she remembered. She remembered every moment of her short-lived marriage with crystal-clear clarity. She had called him that the week before she had left him, her misery getting the better of her. It wasn't where he had come from that had bothered her. It was what he represented to him because of it that had shattered her heart.

"Why? Even *you* can see, after everything you have set in motion, how much Alex loves my sister."

He circled the pillar and neared her, frowning. "And this doesn't bother you at all?"

"What?"

"That the man you had been about to marry is now married to your twin."

"I'm incredibly happy for them. If there's one good thing that's come out of this whole debacle it's Liv and Alex."

"Only one good thing? Still not sure, then?" he queried silkily, his gaze instantly moving to her stomach.

Her spine kissed the steel refrigerator as he suddenly swallowed her space. "Any child who's the product of you and me is of course not a good thing."

"You make it sound like it's a product we designed together."

His words were soft, even amused, and yet they lanced through her. "Excuse me if I'm not the perfect vision of maternal instinct you were expecting."

He stared at her, his gaze searching hers. "Your genes needed a bit of diluting anyway, and you need a bit of softening up. All work and no play makes Kimberly a crabby girl."

"Yes, well—look where all that playing has landed me."

She sucked in a deep breath, sheer exhaustion finally catching up with her. Trust Diego to force her to face the one thing she didn't want to think about.

"We can't even have a conversation without jumping at each other's throats, Diego." Every dark fear she was trying to stay above bled into her words. "How do you think it bodes for the...the child?"

Without looking away from her he pulled her hands from behind her and tugged her gently. Stupefied, she went along, for once lacking the energy to put up a fight. With a hand at her back he guided her to the lounge and pushed her onto the couch.

He settled down on a chair opposite.

She felt the force of his look down to her toes. "You might not want this baby, but you want to do the right thing by it—right?"

She swallowed and nodded, a fist squeezing her chest. It was the only thing she was capable of at this point.

"Good. And, as much as you were hoping that I would walk away, I won't." His gaze was reassuring, his tone comforting. "Believe me, *gatinha,* that's a whole lot more than most kids ever have."

Was it?

Maybe if her mother hadn't left that night…and even when she had maybe if she had at least included Kim… would her life have been different, better, today? No, there was no point in imagining a different past or present. Being weak, trusting her heart, only led to unbearable pain. She had learned that twice already.

"Why are you jealous of Alexander?" The moment the question fell off her lips she regretted it.

His long fingers on his nape, Diego closed his eyes and then opened them slowly. His resentment was clear in the tight line of his mouth. "Alexander King has your confidence. I don't. And, having crawled out of the gutter, I find my first reaction is to hate any man who has what I want."

His stark admission pulled the rug out from under her. "You want my confidence?" She sighed. "How about you stop trying to destroy me for a minute and then we can talk?"

He leaned forward, his elbows on his knees, his expression amused. "Isn't it interesting how your company being in crisis means I'm destroying your life, but when I ruined your wedding you didn't have a word to say? So, did he agree to save your company and thus your *life?*"

His absolutely accurate assumption that her life revolved around her career and her company was beginning to grate on her nerves. She had always prided herself on her unemotional approach. It had been a factor that had put her in direct competition with ruthless businessmen like him.

"No."

He plopped his ankle on his right knee. "Is it because

you deceived him? Have you noticed how you leave *all* the men in your life with less than nice impressions?"

"Not everyone in the world is as concerned about pay-back as you are."

His gaze glittered for a second, but the next he was a rogue, savoring the mess he was making of her life. "So why did Mr. King refuse to be your savior?"

"Because—thanks to your tricks and my own stupid-ity—my image is in tatters. My company is based on the idea of a panel of experts giving women advice on any topic from health, career and fashion to politics, finance and sex. The operative word being *experts*. And, as unfair as it is, a woman who seems to *not* have her personal life together without blemish is not someone others—even other women—want advice from. It doesn't matter that nothing has changed in the way I think or in my brain matter since I learned about my pregnancy. It just is."

"But eventually the news would have come out. I just accelerated it."

He was right. It was something she would have had to face in a couple of months anyway. The sooner she dealt with all this, found a way to resolve this situation with her company, the better.

She still needed an investor, but she was not as worried about running her company as the whole world was. She could do it with her hand tied behind her back.

It was the pregnancy that was the near-constant worry scouring through her.

She had succeeded in everything she had taken up in her life. Pregnancy had to be the same, right?

If she prepared enough, if she was willing to work hard, she could do a good job at being a mother, too. She refused to think about it any other way—refused to give weight to the worry eating away at her from inside.

"What's was the point of all this, Diego?" she said, feeling incredibly tired. "Would it make you feel better if I begged you for help? Leeched money off you in the name of child support?"

"Yes."

She blinked at the vehemence in his answer.

"What I wanted was to scare away all your other investors so that you have no one else to turn to but me."

"Why?"

"It seems putting your company in crisis is the only way for me to get your attention."

Her temper flared again. "That's the second time you have mentioned my success, my company, as though it's something to be sneered at—when you pursued your *own* success with ruthless ambition. And wasn't that why you married me six years ago? Because I was smart, ambitious? Now that I'm pregnant you're asking me to put all that aside and suddenly morph into your vision of everything maternal? I never thought *you* would tout double standards."

Diego ran a hand over his nape. Just the mention of their short-lived marriage was like throwing a punch in his face. She was doing it again—getting under his skin. And it would end in only one way.

"Do you really want to go down the rabbit hole of the past, *gatinha?*"

He didn't want to argue with her. He could see very well that something about her pregnancy was stressing her out. So why didn't she make it easy on herself? If she didn't know how to, he would do it. He would drag her kicking and screaming back into his life and force her to slow down if that was what he had to do to take care of her.

He stepped over the coffee table and joined her on the couch. She scooted to the other corner. He sighed. It seemed either they argued or they screwed, and neither was what he wanted to do. Even if one option had infinitely more appeal than the other.

"I'm not asking you to give up your work. I'm asking you to acknowledge that pregnancy changes things."

Her feet tucked under her, her arms wrapped around herself, she scrunched farther into the corner. She looked absolutely defeated. "And what does *that* entail? Throwing myself a conception party and inviting the whole world?"

"You have no friends, you don't talk to your sister and you're a workaholic. You live in a fortress isolated from anyone else. That cannot continue."

"Keeping myself idle for hours on end with nothing to do is not going to turn me into *mother of the year* when the baby comes. In fact it would just…"

His patience was thinning, but there was something in her voice—a note of desperation—that snagged his attention. "Just what?"

Her stubborn silence was enough to drive his control to the edge again. Was this what he was signing up for a lifetime of?

"I will invest in your company."

Her gaze widened. Her head shook from left to right. "I'll bounce back from this."

"No, you won't." He leaned toward her, and the scent of her caressed him. "Things are different from what they were a week ago."

"Because you manipulated them to your advantage."

"I would have been dead in a ditch years ago if I didn't push things to my advantage." He smiled, enjoying her stupefied silence. "Now I've got you hooked, haven't I? I can see the gears already spinning in your head."

"What's the catch?"

"Aah… Look at us, *gatinha*. We're like an old married couple, reading each other's minds without words. If that's not a true, abiding love, then I don't know what is."

"Stop it, Diego. Why the investment now?"

"Perhaps I don't want to see your hard work go to waste?

Or I'm overcome by a consuming need to help you? I still have a soft spot for my wife?"

Kim shivered as though someone had trickled an ice cube over her spine. His taunts were painful reminders of things she had cherished once and then realized to be false. He was mocking feelings she held close to her heart, emotions she had locked up forever.

"Not funny." With each cheeky retort her anxiety spiraled higher and higher. There *had* to be a huge price to pay for this. "What do you want from me?"

"We make our marriage work. For good."

She jumped from the couch, a chill descending into her veins. He couldn't be serious. It was a twisted joke. That was all it had to be...

She swallowed at the calm in his gaze. "Now I get it. No one is allowed to say no to you, to walk away from you, without you going all *revenge of the ninja* on them. I'm not a task you failed at once and are determined to conquer."

"Let's be very clear about something, *princesa*." The dark humor faded from his gaze, replaced by something hard and flinty. "Putting up with you, tying my life to yours again, is like signing up for a lifetime of torment. But it's a *sacrifice* I'm willing to make for my child. To provide a stable home, to give it everything I didn't have. *Nothing more.* I plan to be a hands-on parent and I will accept nothing less from you."

Bile snuck up Kim's throat. Everything within her rebelled at the thought of being tied to him. It was no better now than it had been six years ago. Then she had been his prize, his trophy, to parade before his father in his victory over a horrible childhood. Now her significance was the fact that she was going to be the mother of his child.

It shouldn't hurt. But it did. And the hurt was followed by the same raking guilt that had taken up permanent residence in her gut.

She couldn't think about what this meant for her. She had to think of the baby. She had to do what was right.

Whether she wanted to be a mother or not, whether or not she felt anything for the life growing inside her, it didn't matter. Unconditional love. She had never received it, she didn't know it, but responsibility and being strong for someone else—that she understood.

"Is this another trick so you can taunt me for the rest of my life? I won't let you use the child as some kind of pawn."

"Every inch of me wants to walk away from you. Every cell in me regrets sleeping with you. I told myself I would not waste another minute on you. But what we did has had consequences. All this is motivated by the fact that we're having a child together. A child who will have a proper father—not one who will just drop in for birthdays and pose for pictures—and a proper mother. A family. I will do everything in my power to ensure my child has everything I never had."

She swallowed, the emptiness she felt exaggerated by his words. In that moment she didn't doubt him.

Diego would do everything for their child. She could see the resolve burning in his eyes. If only he had felt a little of that toward her when they had been married. If only she felt one tenth of the emotion he felt for their child.

"We don't have to be married for that. We could share custody."

"My child is not spending half its life traveling between you and me like a soccer ball. We will be a family—a proper one."

"I'm not sleeping with you."

He laughed—the first sound he'd made that was filled with genuine amusement. "Afraid you won't be able to resist? Don't worry, Kim. I've learned that there are some things in life that can damage even dirty-fighting and wicked me. Like sleeping with you."

"Finally something we agree upon," she said loudly, trying to drown the thundering of her own heart. It figured that now he had caused maximum damage Diego had no interest in her. Why that should bother her of all the things that had happened today was beyond her.

Really, she was becoming a regular passenger on the cuckoo train.

She slid into the couch again, her knees shaking beneath her, trying to grasp the rollercoaster she was signing up for.

"So—a sexless, everlasting marriage to a man who hates me, who owns the biggest share of my company and who will no doubt find unadulterated joy in telling me what a horrible mother I make for the rest of my life? Sounds like a perfect recipe for happily-ever-after."

"Happily-ever-after? Is that what you want, *princesa*? Would you even know it if it bumped you on your overachieving head?"

Hulking over her, he surrounded her, his gaze drilling holes into her.

"For the last time—your company is just a bargaining chip for me. I only ask that you do your best for our child. And as to sex—" his voice lowered to a sinuous whisper, his breath tickling her lips "—if you really want to change that part of the equation we can revisit it—say in a couple of years?" Dark enjoyment slashed the curve of his mouth.

She pulled her gaze upward. The whole situation she found herself in was absurdly comical. If only it wasn't her life. "A reward system? *Great.* Sex for good behavior?"

His mouth curved again, in a smile that dimpled his cheek, pure devilish amusement glittering in it. Her breath stuck in her throat. She had always loved that dimple. On any other man it would have looked effeminate. On Diego it touched his ruthless masculinity with a mischievous charm.

"See—just the way you like it. Everything reduced to a simple business transaction. Be a good little wife and you can have all the sex you want."

CHAPTER FOUR

STANDING IN FRONT of the elevator on her floor, Kim studied herself in the gleaming doors and breathed in gulps of air. So much for her hope that she might be one of the women that Mommy Mary mentioned, who had breezy pregnancies, nesting instincts and glowing skin.

Right.

What she had was nausea, exhaustion, acne—and mood swings as though she had just gotten off of antidepressants. And nothing but an unrelenting detachment at the sight or talk of anything baby-related.

Only a ninety-hour work week, with the added stress of handling PR about the new investment and the expansion of her company, had kept her from spiraling further down.

Two days after he had cornered her in her apartment Diego's legal team had contacted her own. She refused to feed her curiosity by asking where *he* was. Negotiations had been completed in a day and she now had two million dollars to sink her teeth into. It was more than she had expected in her wildest dreams.

She should be overjoyed—she had the investment and she was being awarded the prestigious Entrepreneur of the Year award by the Business Bureau Guild tonight.

But she couldn't turn her mind from thoughts of Diego. It was like a rerun of six years ago, when she had returned to New York, her heart in pieces, wondering if he would call her, if he would come after her...

Not even a month since he'd come back into her life and he was already reducing her to that pitiful self—to someone who signed up for getting hurt so easily.

Maybe she should have accepted Liv's offer to attend the awards ceremony with her and Alex. But she was still avoiding Liv and her well-meaning questions, and arriving with them would only give rise to more of the speculation that was beginning to mess with her head.

Running her company meant she always worked sixteen to eighteen hour days, and that didn't leave time for abiding friendships—or anything else for that matter. It was how she had tailored her life. And she loved it just that way.

Except for the strange tightness in her chest at the thought of the evening ahead, *alone*.

She stepped into the elevator and heard the swish of the doors closing behind her. Leaning her head against the cool mirrored surface of the wall, she fought the tears clogging her throat, a volatile rush of emotion flooding her.

In a way, the threat to her company's expansion had taken her mind off the pregnancy. Now there was nothing to do except face the void inside her. What she wouldn't give to feel one positive thing about this pregnancy...even if it was something as trivial as relief that the nausea was abating.

She reached the front lobby and asked the doorman to hail a taxi. She walked out behind him and pulled her wrap tighter around her shoulders. A black limo came to a smooth stop at the curb.

She stepped out of the way as a chauffeur opened its door. And felt Diego's presence behind her, emerging from her building.

"Ready to go?"

Her heart kicking against her ribcage, she turned around

so quickly that she almost lost her balance. Diego's hand shot out to hold her before she stumbled to the ground.

His arm around her waist, he pulled her to him, enveloping her in a purely masculine scent and hard muscles that made her feel soft all over.

Warmth flooded her, flushing out the inexplicable loneliness of a minute ago. She breathed in a big gulp of air, expanding and contracting her lungs.

Her stomach lurched in an altogether different, pleasurable way. *Why couldn't he make her nausea worse?*

Dressed in a gray Armani suit that hugged his broad shoulders, with his hair slicked back from his forehead, she wondered if he had materialized right out of her thoughts. He exuded raw magnetism, sliding her heartbeat ratcheting up and her already active hormones into overdrive.

His bronzed skin gleamed with vitality in the streetlights, his slightly bent nose and glittering eyes adding to his allure. Languid sensuality cascaded from him.

Even in the chilly New York evening she felt the heat of his perusal on her skin.

"Careful, *pequena,*" he whispered.

A frisson spread in ripples from where his big palm stayed over her back. His grip on her waist tightened as he felt her shiver, the heat from his callused palm singeing her skin through the silk material.

"I know those heels are part of your image but you need to be careful."

She raised her gaze to him, tingling everywhere he touched her. She searched his face hungrily. After his absence for a week she had started believing he regretted his commitment to her—at least the personal part of it.

The moment she found her balance he let her go. As though he didn't want to touch her unless absolutely necessary. Whereas she still tingled everywhere from the briefest of contacts.

"What are you doing here?" she said loudly, trying to speak past the continued boom of her heart.

"I'm coming with you to the awards ceremony."

She closed her eyes and counted to ten, hating herself for the excitement sweeping through her. This was the result of depriving herself of basic human company. This stupid, dangerous thrill at the prospect of an evening with Diego. "Why?"

His smile seemed feral. "To see the whole world praise my wife and fall at her feet for her brilliance."

"Yeah, right. Where exactly did you come from?"

His gaze devoured her, swift and dismissive. "The penthouse."

"The penthouse? What were you doing in the penthouse?" she shot at him, regretting the question the moment she'd said it.

Was he visiting a woman up there? Did she really want to know what Diego got up to in his free time? It had been hard enough to resist gobbling up information about him in the past six years.

"Moving in," he said, with an exaggerated patience that wound her up a little more. "As will you. It will be our home. Until we figure out something more permanent."

"You moved to New York? When? Why?" She refused even to acknowledge the other suggestion he'd slipped in. Equal parts of dread and hope thrummed through her. Because, despite every protest she made with Diego close, the knot in her stomach about her pregnancy relented just a little.

"Why do you think I've moved here?" His mouth twitched. "Have you noticed your brilliance deserts you when I'm around?"

"There's nothing new about that, is there?" She sighed. Really, it was better to accept it than fight it. "For every inch you move closer it's like my IQ drops a few points.

My brain works *sooo* much better with a continent separating us."

He took a step closer and she could smell the scent of his soap and skin combined. Her heart raced. She made a *ca-ching* sound. "Down five points."

His gaze alight with laughter, he ate up a little more of the space between them. She felt the heat of his body tease her skin, tug lower in her belly.

She made another sound with her mouth. Only it emerged croaky and faint this time. "Down five more."

He neared her, tugged at her wrap, which was trailing toward the ground, and tucked it neatly around her bare shoulders. Encompassed by his wide frame, she felt the world around her fall away. His fingers grazed her nape in the barest of touches and lingered. Need rippled across her, every inch of her hyper-sensitive to his nearness.

She wet her lips. "Annndddd...I'll probably spell my own name wrong if you ask me now."

Throwing back his head, he laughed. It was such a heart-felt sound that she couldn't help but smile, too. And marvel at the breathtaking beauty of the man. She felt the most atavistic thrill, like a cavewoman—the very thing she had accused him of being—that he was choosing to spend the evening with her.

He moved away from her, his mouth still curved. "We want you functioning with your normal brilliance tonight, right?"

She should be glad he had some kind of control, because apparently she had none when it came to him. Swallowing her body's frustrated groan, she looked away from him. "Have you really moved to New York?"

He studied her with a lingering intensity. The laughter waned from his face. "Aah...you thought I wasn't coming back."

"I went by your past record." She gave voice to the

thought that wouldn't leave her alone. "Of course I forgot that this time you have something precious to come back for."

He closed his eyes for an infinitesimal moment, his posture throwing off angry energy. When he spoke, his gaze was flat, his voice soft with suppressed emotions. "Are you accusing me of something, *pequena?*"

She shook her head. She was too much of a coward to hear what she already knew—that she hadn't mattered enough for him to come after her six years ago.

With his hand at her back, he nudged her toward the waiting limo.

She settled into the seat, scrambling to get her wits together. Acknowledging that her common sense went on a hike when he was close was something; mooning over him was another. She crossed her legs. Her dress rode up to her thighs and she tugged the fabric down, heat tightening her cheeks. Watching her like a vulture, Diego didn't miss anything. She pulled her wrap tighter and sat straight, like a rigid statue.

One glance in the tinted windows was enough to throw her further equilibrium.

She was due for a haircut, which meant her hair didn't have the blunt look she preferred but curled around her face in that annoying way. And she hadn't had the strength, for once, to straighten it to its usual glossy look. She had applied a little foundation and her usual lip gloss. But she looked pale after another sleepless night. She plumped her hair with her fingers on one side, so that a curl covered it.

She fidgeted in her seat and pulled the edges of her wrap together. *Again.* She should have changed, even if it had meant she would be late. Because the dress just…*clung* too much. The fabric cupped her breasts tight. One could probably even make out the shape of her…

Damn it. Nothing about the evening felt right.

Diego's attention didn't waver from her for a second.

She looked at him and uttered the first thing that came into her head. "Do I look okay?"

"Excuse me?"

"It's a simple question, Diego."

"Really? I didn't think you needed assurance in any walk of life."

"Well, you're wrong. I have lots of moments where I think I might just break," she said, with a catch she couldn't hide, "and this pregnancy is bringing out the worst in every way possible—mood swings, nausea. And you're not making it easy by..."

He pulled her hand into his and squeezed. His touch anchored her—a small but infinitely comforting gesture. "Tell me how I can help."

"For starters you can tell me—" she sucked in a deep breath "—how I look."

His gaze flicked to her, roguish amusement glinting in it. "Okay. Take off that wrap."

Her mouth clamped shut, Kim sat rigid, her hands fisted in her lap.

"Do you want my opinion or not?"

"Yes."

He grabbed the edge of her cashmere wrap and pulled it.

His gaze traveled over her slowly, methodically, from her hair to her shoulders, left bare by the strapless beige silk dress which hugged every curve. She sucked in her breath as it hovered over her midriff.

It felt like forever before it moved to her bare legs and her feet clad in Prada pumps.

He cleared his throat. "You look *different,*" he finally said.

Of course he was going to squeeze the moment for everything. "What kind of different?"

Amusement glinted in his gaze. "Are you fishing for a compliment, *minha esposinha?*"

"Maybe… And stop calling me your wife." She smoothed her hands over her thighs. The soft, lush silk only heightened her anxiety. "This is not me. I much prefer—"

"Conservatively cut clothes that say 'look at my brain, not at my breasts.'"

Did he miss *anything?* "I have to present the right image, work harder than a man for the same level of respect. Not everyone in the business world is as forthcoming as you are with their confidence in my capabilities—much less their…money…" she finished slowly, realizing how much truth there was in her words.

She knew firsthand how ruthless a businessman he was, that the only allowances he made were for hard work. He might have invested in her company in the most twisted way possible, but he hadn't had to. If he'd truly wanted to leave her with no options he could have really let it all go down the drain…

"Thank you for your investment—for your trust in me," she said, trying to breathe past the tightness in her chest.

He shrugged. "Only a fool would doubt your company's success, or your ability to run it whatever your personal life." His gaze moved over her again quickly. "Although I have to tell you it doesn't really work."

She blinked, her skin tingling at his appraisal. "What doesn't?"

He smiled, apparently finding her stupidity very amusing. "Whatever you wear—even those trousers and shirts that you are so fond of—it doesn't hide the fact that you're hot."

Something latent uncoiled in his gaze—a spark—but was gone before the meaning of his words even sank in. How did he do that? How was he so effortlessly able to look at her with so much desire in his eyes and in the next bank it down to nothing?

She stared at his dark head as he powered up his tablet.

She had thought nothing had changed in him in six years. She was wrong. A lot had—and not just his success.

The man she had married had been a passionate twenty-one-year-old, quick to anger and to love. His emotions had simmered on the surface almost like a glow, a blaze of undiluted energy that lured everyone toward him.

His drive to succeed, his determination to squash anything that lay in his way—she had understood *that* ambition. But this new, refined man…he had a disconcerting calm, a control to him, that gave no clue as to what was simmering beneath the surface. Unless he told her with that piercing honesty.

She had expected him to question her about the pregnancy. He hadn't. She had expected him to walk away without a backward glance. He hadn't. And on top of that he was really here, in New York. Because he wanted to give their marriage a real try.

She couldn't get the measure of him because everything she had taken for granted before was now hidden beneath a veneer of sophisticated charm, of polite courtesy.

But she knew the man beneath it, and she didn't buy that façade for a second. If she lowered her guard, if she let him into her life any more than she absolutely had to, she had a feeling he would only strike again. And this time she wouldn't be able to walk away unscathed.

A scowl on his face, he flicked the tablet off. He leaned forward in a sudden movement, his jaw tight. "So, why the change in how you dress?"

She had a feeling he'd meant to say something else—as if he was working to control himself first. "It's a friend's design. I agreed to do her a favor and wear it tonight. Except she tricked me and didn't deliver it until an hour ago. She knew I wouldn't—"

"You wouldn't wear it otherwise? Smart woman," he said. "She knows that the only way to get you to do something for others is to trick you or to manipulate you."

His words pricked her with quiet efficiency. "Is this what you mean by creating a happy environment to raise a kid? Throwing continuous barbs at me? Because I've seen that marriage. I'm a product of that marriage. And, believe me, it only screws up the kids."

She leaned back against the seat, feeling as fragile as a piece of glass. How stupid had she been to believe even for a moment that there could be truce between them? Six years of separation wasn't enough to thaw this anger between them. Or the attraction, for that matter.

"I had...I *have* every intention of making this work."

His words weren't bereft of emotion now. On the contrary, they vibrated with a dark intensity that gave her goosebumps.

"Except you make it so hard to be civilized with you."

"What are you talking about?"

He raised the tablet toward her. "I just watched the coverage of your press statement."

"And?"

"You left out the most important part. *Again.*"

"I don't know what you're talking about. My statement was concise. I followed the details of the investment contract, just as your legal team dictated, and I stopped it from downgrading into Twenty Questions about my personal life."

"Your personal life," he said softly, "is not just yours anymore."

She waited for him to elaborate. Unknown dread pooled in her gut.

The limo came to a stop in front of the plush New York

Plaza Hotel, where the awards ceremony was being held. She could hear the hushed roar of the crowd outside.

Before she could blink he opened a small velvet box.

Drawing a painful breath, she tucked herself farther into her seat, her heart pounding behind her ribcage. He'd done this on purpose—waited until the last minute.

The diamond twinkled in the dark, every cut and glitter of it breathtaking in its princess setting. There was an accompanying band of white gold, exquisitely simple in contrast to the glittering diamond.

Alarm twisted her stomach into a knot. That simple band might very well be an invisible shackle, binding her to him. And it could unlock every impossible hope, every dangerous dream she had so ruthlessly squashed to survive. "I don't want to wear it. I don't know what you think this achieves…"

Her words faltered as he gently tugged her hand into his and slipped the rings on her finger. They were cold, heavy against her skin, yet she felt branded.

"It puts a stop to the dirty speculation about you…about my child."

"What does it matter what the world thinks?"

"Do you know when the first time my mother took me to see my father was?"

Every other thought fled her mind. She just stared at him. She knew he didn't like talking about his childhood. And she hadn't pushed him six years ago.

"I was six. We stood outside his house for three hours before he even met with us. Then she took me again when I was seven. Every year she would drag me to his doorstep, hoping this time he would accept me as his son. I grew up hearing the neighborhood's taunts—*bastard* and so much more. She wanted a different life for me, a better one, but I never cared. I didn't think he owed me anything. Until she ended up in the hospital."

A cloud of dark anger surrounded him in proportion to the incredible cruelty of his father's treatment. A knot twisted in her own gut. Could she blame him for how much he had hated his father? Because she knew, firsthand, what a parent's negligence, even indifference, could do to a child. "How old were you?"

He blinked as though suddenly realizing she was there. "Sixteen. Her body was weakened by years and years of hard labor and not enough food. I couldn't pay for her treatment, and she'd made me promise I wouldn't go back to the street gangs. So I went to see him. By myself for the first time."

Her gut churned, the subdued violence in him raising the hairs on her neck. Sixteen years old—he had been nothing but a child himself. Suddenly she had a feeling where this was going. She understood what had angered him so much. Guilt spiraled through her.

"I went to the offices of his construction company. I begged him to pay for her treatment. I told him I would work for him for the rest of my life. He had his bodyguard drag me by my collar and throw me out. She died that night. And I swore I would take everything from him. I didn't stop until I destroyed him."

"Diego, how would I—?"

"There is very little I have asked of you or will ever ask of you. But when it comes to our child I won't settle. I will never be that boy who was denied his rights ever again." He shrugged—a casual movement, in complete control of himself. "I want my child to be recognized as mine. You had the perfect chance to do that at your press statement. You didn't. So now we will do it my way."

Diego let his fingers linger around Kim's as she stepped out of the limo and joined him on the red carpet in front of the New York Plaza.

He felt her fingers stiffen in his, her body already taut as a tightly wound spring.

For a minute everything around him, all the ruckus, faded away as he let himself indulge in the gloriously sensuous figure she made by his side.

The cream-colored dress drew a straight line, covering her breasts, but it was the sexiest sight he had ever seen. His fingers fanned out of their own volition over her back. The cut of the dress was such that it didn't begin again until the upper curve of her buttock.

Everything in him that was barely restrained roared at the silky feel of her skin.

Desire was a hard knot in his belly, messing with his thinking. As it had been in the limo. It was hard enough to resist her when she dressed in trousers and jackets, even though they didn't hide the sensuality of the woman beneath.

At least *he* had never been able to buy into the frosty business façade. Maybe because he knew the passion that lurked beneath her composed, perfect exterior.

But dressed as she was now, every curve and dip delineated so sexily, her long legs in those heels... He had a better chance of stopping breathing than controlling his hunger for her.

Her wrap slipped and a creamy shoulder glistened in the camera flashlights. A simple chain with a teardrop diamond pendant glittered at the juncture of her breasts. He swallowed, heat flexing in his muscles, pumping him for action, and pulled his gaze away.

A roar erupted around them as they turned together and mounted the carpeted steps. Flashes exploded in their faces, a frenzy of questions in the air around them.

Her press statement about a new investor for her company, against all the odds, had been sensational enough. The fact that it was him hadn't gone unnoticed by the media.

But of course she hadn't answered their questions. Which meant the task was left to him. More fool him that he had believed even for a minute she would do the right thing. That she would give him what he deserved without him having to fight for it.

It was good that he'd fought his whole life for every little thing—from the roof over his head, to every single morsel of food.

He had fought for his mother, he had fought for himself, and now he would fight for his unborn child.

He tightened his grip around Kim as she faltered, her mouth stiff with the smile she'd pasted on, her chin tilted high. It was but a momentary fracture in her perfection, not noticed by anyone but him.

The media were like bloodhounds after her, rejoicing in even a little crack in the pedestal of perfection that Kimberly Stanton stood on.

Nothing would give him more satisfaction than fracturing that pedestal, breaking the woman, so that all of her was undone at his hands. Except it would require a price from him, too, a piece of his soul, and he was damned if he'd let her take anything more from him.

"Ms. Stanton, is it true that you were still married when you were engaged to your twin's husband?"

"Who is the father of your child?"

"Are you seeing Mr. Pereira now?"

Diego heard her startled gasp amidst the rumble and forced her to stop beside him. Had she not expected this? Had she no idea how hungry the media was for a story—*any story*—about her?

He leaned over the thick rope that contained the press, toward the microphones thrust into his face. "It is Mrs. Pereira," he said, and paused, waiting for his words to sink in. He turned toward Kim and smiled. He bent and kissed her cheek. The shock in her gaze was visible only to him.

The softness of her skin burned an imprint on his mouth and he turned toward the flashing cameras again. "And we're very happy to begin our life together again, with our baby on the way."

The crowd went ballistic. He hadn't expected any less.

"You guys are married?"

"Reunited after six years."

He pulled her tighter toward him, every action hungrily raked over by the crowd. She felt like a ticking bomb that could go off at any minute.

"My wife realized her mistake and came back to me on the eve of her wedding."

"You are happy to be together?"

"Incredibly happy," he said, tongue in cheek. "Like we've never been apart."

Kim turned to him, her face devoid of any color. "You bastard," she hissed at him.

He deftly pulled her away from the uproar his statement had caused, dark satisfaction heating his blood. His arms around her slender waist were literally keeping her upright as he and his wife climbed the stairs.

An incredible high buzzed through his veins. Possessive triumph sang in his blood.

His wife.

He had waited for this moment for a long time. To be able to shout to the world that Kim was his wife and have her accept it.

The fact that he had arrived at it through foul means and six years late didn't diminish his victory one bit.

He'd learned a long time ago that playing fair would give him nothing but a bruised body and a broken heart.

CHAPTER FIVE

I<small>T WAS THE</small> worst evening of Kim's life.

It shouldn't have been.

The awards ceremony was being held in the huge banquet hall at the Plaza, the food was delicious and she was rubbing shoulders with great business minds.

Yet in between avoiding Liv's curious gaze, fielding congratulations from her peers, which were *not* over her being chosen for the prestigious award, Kim had never wanted to escape more.

She had realized two minutes after they had walked in that Diego's infuriating statement to the press had given new meaning to the term fairy-tale ending. It wasn't enough that the incredible mockery of his statement—something she would have cherished in an alternative life—haunted her, pricked her.

With the news of his two-million-dollar investment in her company coupled with his revelation that he was the father of her child *and* that they were married, he'd suddenly become her knight in shining armor.

No matter that the same crowd—the same media—had called him a monster just days ago, for his predatory tactics when it came to new businesses, for the way he had recently used a man's gambling losses to take ownership of an island off of Brazil's coast. An ecological paradise, no less, which he was allegedly going to mine and destroy for its precious metals.

Her mouth hurt from the contented smile she forced to her lips as more people congratulated her for the fact that she had landed on her feet with Diego.

She didn't know what infuriated her more—Diego's charming smiles and the intimate glances he threw her way in the face of everyone's prurient curiosity about them, or the educated crowd's insulting joy that she finally had her act together.

As if Diego's very presence in her life could somehow make her brain work better. She laughed at the irony of it.

By the time the awards presentation was over and her speech delivered—which had left a sour taste in her mouth—all she wanted was to escape the crowd, sink into her marble bathtub and lose her mind in a crossword puzzle.

But her torment was nowhere near over yet.

His grip on her wrist unyielding, Diego pulled her onto the dance floor. His hands around her waist, he enveloped her in a hard wall of heat until he filled her vision and the invigorating scent of him was all she could breathe.

He had held her at arm's length ever since she had blurted out the news of her pregnancy. The sudden intimacy of his embrace now toppled her equilibrium, and her flesh sighed against his hardness.

Her skin tingled when his callused fingers moved over her back at images and sensations she'd rather not remember: the feel of those calluses on the sensitive skin of her thighs, the muscles in his back bunching under her fingers… Her body reveled in the memories his nearness evoked.

She sucked in a sharp breath, willing herself not to melt into his arms, not to enjoy it so much. Because all this was for show. He was playing to the media, leaving no doubt in anyone's mind about them, leaving her no way out.

At least no way out with her life still intact.

He studied her, curious amusement playing on his mouth. "You're not enjoying the evening?"

She pulled her head back and glared at him. "I've never been more disappointed in my entire life. I'm the same person with the same faculties I had yesterday. And yet *you* get lauded for sweeping me off my feet."

A smile curved his lush mouth, and infuriated her further.

"You weren't this upset even when I trapped you at the island."

"I don't like being thought an incompetent idiot," she said, gritting her teeth.

His mouth narrowed with displeasure. "You mean you don't like even the *illusion* that you're in love? You have your investment, your company's reputation is intact and you have my total support with the pregnancy. I don't see what's bothering you so much."

Put like that, she sounded the very epitome of selfishness. But she couldn't quiet the increasing panic that things were slowly but surely slipping out of her control. That Diego was stripping away everything she needed to survive. Whatever his intentions, the truth was that he would bring her down to her knees, plunge her into the same whirlpool of crippling hope, if she wasn't on guard.

"There's no need for this pretense that we're living a happily-ever-after. As if this is *Romeo and Juliet Reunited.*"

"No? Have you thought of how this might have affected your sister and her life? Being continually mobbed by the media speculating on how she felt about her sister carrying her husband's child?"

Her mouth fell open. "Liv always knew the truth."

"Does it mean it doesn't bother her? Hurt her? Cast a dirty shadow on her marriage? What about Alexander King? You went straight to him for help, and you claim guilt for having deceived him, but did you think for a minute what this twisted speculation might do to him? Do you care that you've asked them to pay a high price just because it raises your hackles to be tied to me?

Shame flooded her within, and her gaze wavered away from him. God, every word out of his mouth was true. She had been avoiding Liv, worried she would know that Kim was barely keeping it together.

"Did you give a moment's thought to me? Or have you, in your usual selfish fashion, neglected to think of anyone else but you?"

"How would I know how you felt about this? Until a couple of hours ago I didn't know how cruelly your father had treated you, or how your mother died. You never told me anything. Once we were off that ship you kept me in a bubble, as if…" She met his gaze, the disbelief spiking there halting her words.

But would she have behaved differently even if she had known?

He frowned, and she had a feeling he was thinking the same.

"The truth is that it scrapes at you that you're not able to reduce this pregnancy and my involvement in it into something tangible." Frustration glimmered in his gaze. "Anything that makes an average woman happy breaks *you* out in hives."

"Your fault if you thought me average."

"No, I didn't think you average—or this warped either. You cover it all up with your perfection."

She mocked a pout, her heart crawling into her throat. Only Diego could reach the horrific truth with a few careless words. The muscles in her face hurt with the effort to keep the smile intact, even though inside everything had crumbled under his attack.

But she couldn't let him or their marriage mean anything

to her. He had already proved her worst fear true once. If she let her guard down, if she let herself care, she would just break this time. "Does that mean you don't want a perfect wife anymore?"

His fingers tightened over her hipbones, a fierce scowl bunching his forehead. "You're the one obsessed with perfection. Not me. And I never wanted a perfect wife either."

"You mean *now?*"

"What?"

"Now that you've achieved all this status, this wealth, now that you've proved yourself to your father and the whole world, you don't need a trophy wife for an accessory *now.* Not like you did six years ago."

His hand stole up her back, his fingers curling possessively around her nape. Her skin seared as though branded. The entire world around them fell away in that moment. As did the veneer of his sophistication. A curse fell from his lips and she colored. Even her little grasp of Portuguese was enough for her to understand.

"You don't want to wear my ring. You didn't want to acknowledge the baby as mine. However much I want to give this marriage a try, you're determined to make this warfare. Maybe working sixteen-hour days with no social life is beginning to fry your brain and corrupt your memories."

He whispered in her ear. It was a low growl, every word pulsing with the slow burn of his anger.

"Because I was not the one that walked away. You knew when you married me what I came from. When we got off the cruise, when the dirty reality of my roots, my life, began to creep in, you didn't want me anymore. So don't you *dare* blame me for the past."

Diego set Kim away from him, his muscles pumping with furious energy. He needed to walk away right that moment, before he did something stupid.

Like kissing her senseless or driving his fist into the nearest wall.

This was the woman who had looked back at him calmly after he'd slept with her and then discarded her as if she was garbage. This was the woman who had then quietly slunk back to her life, to her waiting fiancé, calmly dismissed any thought of him and gone on with her life.

Nothing touched her—not the fact that he was back, not the fact that she was carrying his child. How many times did he need to learn the same lesson?

How *dared* she place the blame for their failed marriage at his feet?

And yet he could swear he had seen sadness lurking in her eyes as she had called herself a trophy wife, felt her shiver as if her words were leaching out the warmth.

He was about to walk out of the hall, away from the crowd, when someone tapped him on the shoulder. He turned around, his control razor-thin.

Beautiful brown eyes—open, smiling, similar to Kim's and yet so different—greeted him. *Olivia King.*

She wore a red knee-length dress. A ruby pendant hung at her neck. Where Kim's hair was cut into a sophisticated blunt style, Olivia's hair was long and curly and wild. There was nothing drastically different from the way Kim was dressed, especially tonight in a dress uncharacteristic of her. And there was the same sensuous vitality to Olivia that was muted but so much more appealing in Kim.

"Hello, Diego," she said, with very little hesitation in her expression.

He raised a brow at her familiarity. She waved a hand at him and moved closer. The gesture, her very movement, lacked the grace and the innate poise he expected from that face. It stunned him into a moment's silence.

"Sorry to be crowding you on the dance floor like this, but I have to take my chance now. You're the father of my niece or nephew—" a smile split her mouth "—and I only have a few moments before Alexander chews my head off for butting in."

His anger thawing, Diego took the hand she offered boldly.

Where Kim wore her sophistication, her brilliance, like an armor that no one could pierce, Olivia's irreverence, her open smile, was the pull. Her emotions were right there in her smiling gaze.

A man wouldn't look into those eyes and wonder if she was his salvation or his purgatory. He wouldn't have to spend a lifetime wondering if he was banging his head against a rock.

They looked exactly the same and yet were so different. He found it highly disconcerting and illuminating. Because he didn't feel the least bit of attraction toward her.

He frowned. "A chance at what, Mrs. King?"

Her gaze twinkled. "Call me Liv. My chance to talk to you. Everyone's talking about your statement to the press, and Kim hasn't been very…forthcoming about you."

"No?" Just like that his ire rose again. "Let's just say I'm your perfect sister's dirty little secret."

His gaze sought the woman in question and found her immediately. Kim was standing at a table, talking to Alexander.

They were peas in a pod, those two. So similar in everything. And yet Alexander King had walked away from Kim, entrenched himself in scandal for Olivia.

"Which you've made sure is not a secret or dirty anymore," Olivia said, with the initial warmth fleeing from her words.

He flicked his gaze back to her. "Waiting for your sister to do the right thing was a futile exercise."

A little frown appeared in her brow. "My sister…" She

hesitated, as though choosing her words carefully. "She's always kept her feelings and her fears to herself."

"You mean she *has* any under that brilliance?"

Her brow furrowing, Olivia continued, "Kim always had to be the strong one—for my mother and for me. It was the only way to survive—the only way she could protect me."

"From whom?" he said, before he could stop himself. He rubbed his nape, feeling tension curl into his muscles. Damn his wife and his ever-spiraling curiosity about her. "You know what? All I care about is that she does the right thing by my child."

He couldn't keep his resentment out of his words.

Olivia nodded. "Look, all I wanted to say was that I'm glad you and Kim are working things out."

"Do you know, if looks could kill, I would have died a few times from your husband's wrath in the past few minutes?"

She glanced to where they stood—her husband and his wife. "Please ignore Alexander." She bent toward him, and though she stood at a perfectly respectable distance to someone standing on the other side of the room, it looked as though she was too close to Diego. "He's a bit possessive when it comes to me."

She had sidled closer to him just to get a rise out of her husband. On cue, the frown on the other man's brow deepened across the banquet hall. Diego smiled despite everything. "He doesn't like me very much."

She smiled. "My husband has a very rigid sense of right and wrong."

"*Really?* And yet he carried on with you while pretending to be married to her? Traded her for you without a moment's—?"

Her gaze flashed with anger. "Alexander and Kim—what they shared was not a real relationship. Even before she knew about us, after her time with you on the island, she broke it off with him. I mean, they never even—"

Kim had broken it off with Alexander? When? He felt as though he'd had his breath knocked out of him. "Never even what, Olivia?"

Olivia's look was more calculated now, gauging if he was trustworthy. "Did you mean what you said to the press? About a new beginning with Kim?"

"Yes."

"Alexander and Kim never had a physical relationship."

Diego felt as if a curtain was falling away from his eyes. Primal satisfaction filled his veins even as he wondered why his perfect wife would hide something like that from him. Especially when he had accused her of being unemotional and unaffected by how easily she had gone back to Alexander.

But of course Kim offered nothing of herself. Truth or anything else. Frustration erupted through him.

True, he had given her the perfect reason to believe him the enemy. And that had to change if their marriage had a chance of being anything but a battleground.

He looked up at Olivia just as she stiffened next to him. Within seconds the color fled from her animated face and her gaze was stricken with fear. Diego turned to see where her gaze was trained.

Their father, Jeremiah Stanton, was shaking hands with someone.

His gaze instantly zeroing on his wife, Alexander cut his way across the crowd toward them, his stride purposeful.

Even Diego felt a flash of anxiety at the fear that filled Olivia's eyes. "Olivia? Are you all right?"

She glanced up at him, her gaze glittering with pain. "Sorry. Old habits die hard." She bent toward him, the very picture of anxiety. "You have to find Kim immediately— okay?"

"What are you talking about?"

"My father," she said, glancing at him and turning away quickly. "I know his wrath when he's displeased better than anyone. He won't like what the media's been saying about her."

"I don't either."

"You don't understand. He will rip into her for this. Whatever issues you have with her, tonight just…just take care of her."

Her muscles quivering, Kim paced the quiet corner of the banquet hall.

Every inch of her wanted to confront Diego, challenge every arrogant word he had uttered about six years ago. She could take anything he tossed at her—his tactics to control her company, his manipulations. But she couldn't stand his latest accusations. His background had never bothered her—not then, not now. As if she had *ever* assumed that she was better than him, as if she hadn't given it *everything* she had in her—until he had turned her into his prize trophy.

She turned toward the banquet hall, determined to have it out with him right there. And then she saw her father at the edge of the crowd, walking toward her, wearing the fiercest scowl she had ever seen.

With her father being out of country for the past month she had almost forgotten about him. They hadn't had their twice-weekly lunch, and of course he had only flown in today. Which meant this was the first he'd be hearing about everything.

She smiled as he neared her, a feeling of failure threading through her. She ran a hand over her stomach, unable to stop herself. Anger fell off him in dark waves. Which wasn't unusual—except before it had always been targeted at Liv.

She bent her cheek toward him as she always did, but he

didn't kiss it. Straightening up, she met his gaze. The fury pulsing in it curled into dread in her stomach.

"Have you lost your goddamned mind, Kimberly?" His words were low and yet his wrath was a tangible thing around them. "I'm gone for a month and not only have you screwed up your life, but your company too?"

She drew a sharp breath in. "Dad, I understand how awful this must sound to you, but I'm trying my best to control the damage. I'm so sorry you had to hear about it like this."

"Are you? Wherever I turn I'm smacked in the face with news that both my daughters are indiscriminate..." His gaze flicked to her. "Are you really no better than Olivia?"

She shook her head, hating the disappointment in his words. "For the last time —Liv did nothing wrong. And, yes, I know that I've messed up, but the truth is that I—"

"Unless you can tell me that everything I've heard so far is false there's nothing you can say."

His gaze flayed her, eroding her already thin composure.

"You run away from your wedding, you get yourself pregnant by God-knows-who... After everything I taught you you've proved that you're no better than the trash your mother was. These are *not* the actions of the daughter I raised—the daughter I've always been proud of."

Her heart sinking to her feet, Kim clutched at his hands. She was *not* like her mother. She was *not* weak. "He's not just someone I picked up, Dad," she said, for the first time acknowledging that very fact to herself, too. She had walked away from the hurt Diego had caused her six years ago, given up on a foolish dream, but it didn't mean she was impervious to his sudden reappearance in her life.

"Is it true, then?"

"What?"

"You married him six years ago? He's the father of your...*child?*"

She nodded. "Diego is the baby's father. And, yes, our marriage is valid."

"Then you'd better work it out with him and clean up this mess. The last thing I want is a bastard grandchild."

She flinched at his cutting words. "I will, Dad. I promise. Will I see you—?"

He shook his head, his denial absolute. "Don't call me until you've kept yourself out of the news for a while. And if you can't clean it up you're just as dead to me as your sister is."

Nodding, Kim sagged against the wall as he walked away without a backward glance. She exhaled a long breath, tears prickling behind her eyes. It had to be the damned hormones again. Because her father's reaction should not be a surprise. She had seen it enough times with Liv.

She had let so many people down recently—Liv, Alex, her father *and* herself. Apparently Diego was the only one who didn't care about the consequences. She turned her head and saw him standing there, watching her father go, rage mirrored in his golden gaze.

Diego couldn't believe his own eyes. His ears rang with those softly delivered yet harsh words. It was nothing a father should ever say to his child, and Diego himself had had more than his share of nasty words from his own father.

His temper frayed to the edge. Every inch of him wanted to turn around, find Jeremiah Stanton and pound his fists into the older man.

In another lifetime he wouldn't have given it another thought. He would have worked through his fury the only way he knew how. But he was not that man anymore. He had promised his mother that he would remove the violence that had been part of his life for so long as a member of a street gang.

Even though keeping his promise was the hardest thing at moments like this.

Kim looked frazzled. Her dress had more color than her face. He wrapped a hand around her shoulders and the shocking thing was that she let him. He felt her shiver and a curse fell from his lips. "Are you okay?"

Her brown eyes drank him in silently. The very absence of hurt in them jarred through him. "I'm perfectly fine."

"You were apologizing to him while he uttered the foulest words and yet you flay me for lesser sins?"

He felt her smile against his arm. Holding her like this was pure torture but he couldn't let go.

"That's just the way my father is."

He reared back, frowning. "He laid into you in the middle of a crowd. For what? Because you slept with me? Because you're pregnant? Because you let your control slip for one night? You're twenty-five, you're the CEO of your own company." He frowned as another thought came bursting in. "Are you saying he's always been like this?"

"Yes, but it was usually aimed at my mother and then Liv."

His breath left him in a sharp hiss. "But not you? Ever?"

"I never gave him the chance—never let him find fault with me. I did everything he asked me to and I excelled at it."

"So you're not upset?" he said, disbelief ringing through him.

"I'm upset that I gave him any reason. But you already know that I regret my actions four weeks ago."

"You're *defending* him?"

"My father is responsible for all the success I have achieved. If he hadn't continually pushed me, I would have—I would *be*—nothing. This is his way of warning me to not let it all go down the drain."

"You make one mistake—*if* it can be called that—and he tears you apart? Don't you see—?"

"You're reading too much into this, Diego."

Her mouth was a study in resignation that mocked his anger.

"I've always known that his approval comes with conditions."

"I saw fear in Olivia's eyes. Are you saying he didn't put it there?"

She glanced past him, her gaze riddled with anxiety. "Yes, he did," she said. "Do you know where she is?"

Fisting his hands, Diego reined in another curse. She wasn't upset for herself but for her twin. "Alexander's with her."

"I always tried my best to protect Liv," she said, with a hint of pleading in her tone, as if she needed to explain herself. "The only way to do that was to play peacekeeper by not giving him any more reason to lose it."

Why was it her job to protect Olivia? He kept those words to himself through sheer will. "So of course you had to become everything perfect?"

"Why do you say that like it's a—" she glared at him "—curse? How is he any different from you?"

"Your father is a bully of the worst sort," he said through gritted teeth. "I fought in street-gangs, yes, but I used my fists for survival. If that's what you think about me—"

"No. I didn't mean that you're a bully." She looked at him, her expression pleading. "I meant he's no different from anyone else in his expectations of me. He's just upfront about it. My accomplishments, my capabilities, are the things that draw people to me. Nothing else..." She swallowed, as if she found it hard to speak the words. "It's why you married me six years ago, it's why Alex picked me for his wife and it's what my father's approval of me is based on."

There it was again—that accusation. As though he hadn't...

She swayed and he caught her, questions tumbling through his head.

His throat felt raw at her matter-of-fact admission. But buried beneath it there had been... *hurt.* Her attachment to her company, her isolated lifestyle... Suddenly his perspective shifted, as though he had been looking at her until now through a dirtied window.

"I think I've had enough excitement for the night," she said softly, puncturing his thoughts. Her fingers clasped his arm. "Can we leave?"

He nodded and guided her toward the exit, his palm staying on her back. He couldn't tear his gaze from her, however.

She looked breathtakingly beautiful, every curve and dip of her sexy body outlined in that damned dress, every step she took grace embodied.

Whether it was her disconcerting statement, or the weary look in her eyes, he didn't see the aggravatingly prickly woman she had become.

Instead she reminded him of the night he had met her, on the cruise ship six years ago. The memory stole through him like an insidious drug, catching him unawares.

She had been standing alone on the deck, away from the rest of the crowd. Wind had been whipping her hair; her green knee-length dress had been molded against her slender figure.

None of the usual festivities that attracted a nineteen-year-old—dancing or drinking—had grabbed her interest. She had looked utterly alone, heart-wrenchingly alluring, driving every dormant instinct of his to the surface. He had observed her for over an hour before he had approached her.

They had done no more than exchange their names that night, but he had spent over two hours teasing a smile from her. And when she had smiled he had found the most thrilling, satisfying joy in it. He had felt on top of the world.

That was how she looked now.

Infinitely fragile and unraveled, as if the tiniest pressure might splinter her perfection apart. She *was* hurt by her father's outbursts, though for the wrong reasons.

That flash of vulnerability shredded the anger and scorn with which he had covered up his desire. He had only deceived himself that it was all gone. Need and something more sinuous glided through his veins.

He wanted to grab her by those dainty shoulders and shake her until she realized she didn't need her father's approval, conditional or otherwise. He wanted to kiss her just as much as he wanted to provoke her, until her beautiful eyes sparkled with that infuriating combination of logic and desire. But he couldn't—not if he wanted to keep his sanity intact.

He couldn't fight the feeling that he knew very little about the woman he had married six years ago. Her statement that what she'd represented to him was the reason why he had wanted her pricked like a thorn in his side.

What if there was more to why she had left him? Was he culpable too? And, if he was, why didn't the aggravating woman call him on it?

CHAPTER SIX

KIM SLID FROM the luxurious bed in Diego's spare bedroom—or one of the *six* spare bedrooms. She cast a glance toward the digital alarm clock on the nightstand. It was only five minutes past seven.

Diego's housekeeper, Anna, had mentioned a pool out on the terrace. She needed to burn off some of her restless energy.

Walking into the closet, which was the size of her living room, she searched for her swimsuit. By the time Kim had returned from work the day after she had moved in, Anna had unpacked everything for her.

Spotting the trendy one-piece she had bought recently, Kim tugged off her pajamas and tank top.

She knew why she felt so restless. Coordinating her move into Diego's penthouse to be when he was out of the country had felt like the best idea. Except now she couldn't dwell on anything else.

Would he be pleased? What if he had changed his mind? She had been on tenterhooks for days after the awards ceremony, waiting for him to manipulate something, anything, in order to get her to move.

But he had surprised her with a strangely disappointing silence.

His words at the awards ceremony wouldn't leave her alone, though. Neither had she been able to get Liv's face, when she had waylaid her on the steps of the Plaza, out of her head. Liv had clutched at Kim's hand, concern pinching her mobile mouth.

Her every action, every word, since she had learned of her pregnancy had been directed by the selfish need to protect herself, to make sure she didn't reveal the slightest weakness in front of Diego. She had conveniently pushed Liv away, refused to share anything, uncaring of how worried she might be.

When had she stopped caring about everyone else's feelings along with her own? When had the lines between being strong and selfishness blurred? Would she continue to push Diego away because he was the one man who had the power to hurt her, to drive her to weakness?

Would she do that when she had the child too? Would she put her own well-being first always? Would she put herself before her child as her own mother had done?

The questions had tied her up in knots. So before she lost her nerve and remembered the million reasons why it was a bad idea she had called Anna and informed her she was moving in.

She pulled her robe on and pushed her feet into comfy slippers. It took her a few minutes of walking through the long corridor to reach the lushly carpeted foyer.

She reached the grand salon and sighed. Huge pillars stood in the room, supporting high ceilings. The room could have housed her entire apartment. Pristine white marble floors gleamed beneath her slippered feet, and the glass walls all around offered three-hundred-and-sixty-degree views of midtown Manhattan and the southern end of Central Park.

Contemporary art graced the walls. She smiled as she recognized a couple of artists native to Brazil.

It was the spectacular luxury she had expected from a man with Diego's assets, and yet it was different. There was no ostentation here or anywhere else in the penthouse. Just a quiet, simmering elegance—a flash of bright red here and there, a candid portrait of a street-fighter on the streets of Rio de Janeiro reflecting Diego's passionate nature.

The best feature, however, was that it was so big she needn't ever see Diego unless required.

Feeling a lightness that had been missing for several weeks, she walked through the salon toward the terrace.

She stepped into the covered part of the L-shaped space and a shape emerged from the shadows. She had expected it to be only Anna and her for another night.

A quiet gasp escaping her, she stepped back. A teen-ager, his bulging biceps inked with elaborate tattoos, one of which looked eerily familiar, met her gaze. Her mouth fell open as he moved toward her and the light from the salon behind her illuminated his face.

The left side of his rugged face was covered in blue and purple bruises. His hair was cropped close to his scalp. A naughty smile split his severely cut mouth, which had blood crusted on it. "You are Diego's wife?"

Between his thick accent and his swollen lip Kim was barely able to understand him. She nodded, a different kind of shiver overtaking her now.

He stepped in front of her when she moved, leaving only just enough space between them. His gaze traveled over her leisurely in a defiant, purposeful scrutiny that she assumed was meant to make her nervous.

With every inch of her headspace taken up by thoughts of Diego, she wasn't.

"I'm Miguel," he said, still sporting that smile, which was just short of lascivious. "If you get...*bored* with Diego..." He finished his sentence with a wink and a sub-tle thrust of his hips that left no doubt in her mind. "Call me. I will treat you right."

She stood stiffly without blinking. "Nice to meet you,

Miguel," she threw at him, refusing to show how much his presence had spooked her.

She stepped onto the rooftop terrace, her head spinning with questions—which fled her mind at the sight in front of her.

The vast terrace was illuminated with little solar lights lined up against the floor. The rest of the light came from the spectacular skyscrapers of Manhattan around them. The effect was breathtakingly simple and just the peace she wanted.

There was a fire pit with comfy-looking recliners to her left, and a small bar with a glass top. But it was the perimeter of the pool that caught and held her attention.

A hot tub was on one side, with a couple of loungers on the other.

She walked toward the pool like a moth drifting to light—until the splash-splash of long, powerful strokes punctured the silence.

It took her a moment to realize that half the pool stretched past the terrace, overhanging the streets of New York. Her heart thudded like a tribal drumbeat, her gaze searching for the powerful figure in the water.

Not that she needed to see him to know that it was Diego. Only *he* could find swimming in a pool that edged twenty stories into the sky relaxing.

She was about to turn around, ready to flee, when he swam to the edge of the pool facing her and stood.

His wet hair clung to his scalp, outlining the strong angles of his face. Water sluiced enticingly over biceps that flexed while holding him up. His gaze ran over her, sweeping thoroughly from the top of her mussed hair to the opening of her robe and her bare legs. "Is everything okay?"

She folded her arms around her midriff. "Yes, everything's fine. I just…"

"Did you come up for a swim?"

"What? No. I....." She clasped the sash of her robe, moving to the balls of her feet, ready to run.

She sighed. This was her reality now. Seeing Diego in all his glorious forms, apparently counting up her points on his weird reward system for sex. She smiled at the absurdity that she was actually keeping count.

How desperate was she?

"I did come for a swim," she said, trying hard to keep her gaze on his face. And not trail down his wet, sexy body. "But not from my own apartment."

He pushed at the water dripping from his forehead with his hand. His frown grew. "From where, then?"

"Didn't Anna tell you? I moved in when you went to... Well, wherever it is that you went."

Luckily he didn't seem to have noticed the curiosity in her words.

With an agility that was a beauty to watch he pulled himself up in a single movement. And of course he was naked.

She gasped and closed her eyes. But the sight of his chest and midriff, velvet skin rippling over toned muscles, was etched into her mind. A twang shot through to her sex. She squeezed her thighs—which didn't help at all.

The man was knock-your-knees-out-from-under-you sexy. Was it any wonder he'd always been able to scramble her senses as easily as he did?

"You can open your eyes now."

She did.

A white towel was wrapped low on his hips. He walked around the pool, reaching the bar on her right in silence. The muscles in his back moved sinuously as he poured himself a drink and quickly guzzled it down.

A faint hum began thrumming over her skin. Even the thin silk of her robe felt oppressive.

The tattoo on his back, right under his shoulderblades, glimmered under the low lights. A memory rose to the surface, heating her already warm skin. She had traced that ink with her fingers first and then with her tongue, fascinated by the ripple and play of his muscles at her actions.

Six years on she shivered as sensations from that long-forgotten night touched her just as powerfully.

She moved without realizing it to where he stood, and ran a finger over the wing of the eagle.

He jerked, the muscles in his back bunching tight. As if she had touched him with a hot poker. He faced her before she could blink, his scowl fierce.

She jerked her hand back. "That tattoo…" She licked her lips, her cheeks tightening, "That eagle shape… The teenager I just met—he has—"

Suddenly he was so close that she could smell the scent of him, see the evening stubble on his jaw, feel the warmth of his body. His scowl deepened. "Miguel?" He looked back inside. "Did you run into him? Did he say anything wrong to you?"

"Not really," she said, hurrying to reassure him. "I just didn't spot him until he stepped out of the dark. I didn't know anyone else was here, or that you were back."

His frown grew. He moved away from her, his movements edgy. "Anything more?"

She shook her head belatedly.

Heat unfurled in the pit of her stomach as he turned to the side, dropped his towel casually and pulled up a pair of black sweatpants. She caught a glimpse of tight butt and rock-hard thighs.

Her heart raced. The stretchy fabric of her swimsuit was chafing everywhere it touched. She needed that swim even more than before.

He turned around to face her, his expression serious. With his glorious rippling chest close enough to touch, it was hard to focus on his face.

"I'll arrange something else for him. He's already upset

Anna in the few hours he's been here. Probably why she forgot to mention you were here. He won't harm you, but I know how nervous you get around people from that background."

Hurt splintered through her, knocking the breath out of her. Maybe it was because she hadn't been prepared to see him tonight. Maybe it was her hormones again. She glared at him, finding it hard to speak. "Did I say that?" Her words rang in the silence. "I wouldn't even have mentioned him if you weren't flashing that tattoo. I knew this was a bad idea. You might have the best intentions, but you'll never—"

"Wait." His long fingers clasped her wrist and pulled her to him.

She fell into him with a soft thump that made her sigh. Her fingers landed on his chest. The thump-thump of his heart was as loud as her own. He was hard and hot and all she wanted to do was curl into him. Even when he flayed her with his words.

She closed her eyes, lacking the strength not to care about his opinion.

"I didn't mean to upset you." He pulled her chin up and she opened her eyes. His hands on her waist were a languid weight, searing her. "This is our home and I want you to feel safe and be happy here."

Something warm and gooey bloomed inside her chest. She took a deep breath as if she could capture it there. A tingling warmth spread through her—something she remembered from the cruise. For the first time in her life she had felt cherished.

His fingers lingered on her cheek. "The last time our marriage fell apart it was just us." Just as easily he took the warmth away. "This time we have someone else to think of… Do you understand?"

She nodded, swallowing her disappointment. She strove to sound just as casual as he did. "It doesn't bother me. This place is so huge anyway I don't have to even see you if I don't want to, right?" His expression didn't relax. "And... thanks for thinking of me."

He was right. This wasn't about what either of them wanted.

At his quick nod, she grabbed his wrist. The hair on his forearms tickled her fingers. "I appreciate your support since I...since we found out about the—" she needed to stop choking on the word *baby* "—the pregnancy. You've been...great about it, and I...well, I haven't."

His gaze moved to her mouth and lingered. The need to feel his mouth on hers, the need to touch him, rose inside her.

It wasn't the blaze of lust that had driven reason from her head a few weeks ago. Now it was more of a slow, soft burn that always smoldered beneath her skin. It was an insidious longing more dangerous than pure lust.

He extracted his hand from hers as though he couldn't wait to get away. Her heart sinking to her toes, she suddenly realized she wanted his company. Just for a few more minutes. Even if it meant prolonging her own torment.

So she said the first thing that popped into her head. "What happened to Miguel's face?"

He stopped and turned around, surprise flickering in his gaze. Was her interest in the teenager, in what went on in Diego's life, so shocking? *Really,* she wasn't the one with corrupt memories of their short marriage.

"It was his initiation into a street-gang last week. With everything else going on I wasn't able to stop it."

Because he had been dealing with *her.* "He's got the same tattoo as you do. Is it the same street-gang you were a part of?"

For a second the same sensuous memory of that long-ago night flared in his gaze, the pupils turning molten gold. "Yes," he said, in that clipped *whatever* tone of voice.

Turning away from her, he grabbed a white tee shirt and pulled it on. It was a silent version of *show over, move on.*

Something within her rebelled. His calm dismissal was beginning to annoy the hell out of her. Before he could walk away she moved closer to him, effectively blocking him.

"So you got him out of the street-gang?"

"Yes—kicking and screaming."

"He didn't want to come with you?"

He shook his head. "What I forced him to leave behind is the only life he knows. And I need to keep an eye on him. Like I said, he won't harm you. But he's got a grudge against me."

She slid to a lounger and crossed her legs. "Now it all makes sense."

He plunked down on the one next to her. "What do you mean?"

She felt him still and hid a smile. Perverse satisfaction filled her. He wasn't as unaffected by their situation as he made out. "Of course at first I thought it was…you know…the appeal of the *sexy older woman* and all," she said, tongue-in-cheek. She was rewarded by his begrudging grunt. "But now I see it was partly to get back at you. Although I have to admit even with half his face covered in bruises he's quite the looker. He made me a very interesting offer."

He pounced on her like a predator on his prey. One minute they were sitting on two separate loungers, the next he was on hers, his muscular thighs on either side of her, trapping her neatly. His broad shoulders filled up her vision. The very air she breathed was filled with the scent of him.

"You said he didn't say anything." His words were a low growl.

"I meant he didn't say anything threatening."

"What *did* he say to you?"

Diego had been like this with her before, too. And, for

all the time she had spent learning to be self-sufficient, his protective attitude had had her melting like butter under the sun. She smiled, just enjoying the moment. "Stop acting all grouchy caveman over the fact that he talked to me and I will tell you."

Diego closed his eyes, gripped the edge of the lounger and counted to ten. On two he remembered her laughing face. Five—her long, bare, toned legs. On eight the silk robe clinging to her skin, ending several inches above her knees. The luscious picture she made was etched onto his retinas.

Meu Deus, the temptation she presented—walking around his home, making his space her own—was more than he could handle tonight. Even though it was exactly what he had asked her to do.

His trip to Rio de Janeiro, seeing his half brother in the clinic—just a shell remaining of the boy he had once been—it beat down on him like a relentless wave determined to drown him. He knew what to expect, and yet every time the sight of Eduardo kicked him in the gut.

Now he had Miguel to contend with, too. He really couldn't afford to make mistakes in handling the teenager.

And throw in his enticingly sexy wife—parading in a swimsuit, no less—he knew where he would slip up.

He must have truly misplaced his marbles to have suggested that she move in, to think that he could keep his libido in check with her under the same roof.

He would see her in the mornings, all mussed up and unraveled, the way he liked her best. And before he went to bed. The sensuous scent of the woman would be absorbed into every inch of his living space. He hoped his child appreciated the torture he was going through for his or her sake.

"Diego?"

Her voice in front of him was tentative, testing, her fingers on his infinitely tempting. He swallowed a groan. The mischievous note in her voice was gliding like velvet over his skin.

Drawing another bracing breath, he opened his eyes. "Tell me what he said."

"Something about calling him if I ever got bored with you."

"It's not a joke, *gatinha*. Women, like bikes and land, are possessions jealously guarded in that world. Coming onto you is a challenge thrown at *me*."

She frowned, studying him with interest. "But you were from the same background and you never treated me like that. In fact it was the oppo…" Her gaze flickered to him, wary.

Something tightened in his chest. "How *did* I treat you?"

The slender line of her shoulders trembled. "Like I was a princess."

"And yet you…?"

No. He didn't want to turn this into a battle again.

"That was my mother's doing," he said. "Any little good I have in me, she gave it to me. By the time I was ten I had seen how horribly my father treated her, as if life wasn't hard enough for her as a single mother. She would have peeled my hide if I was anything but respectful toward a woman."

Laughter lit up her eyes. "I would have loved to see that."

Her smile wound around him. He couldn't breathe for a second. "And *you*… I could never…"

"What?" She scooted closer and clutched his hands. "Please tell me."

He brought her hand to his mouth and kissed the palm. The scent of her tickled his nostrils. "That cruise… I went on it to amuse Eduardo. You were like this exquisite gift that somehow landed in my lap. That first week I was even afraid to touch you. I was terrified that I would somehow mar you."

She shied her gaze away from him, but not before he saw the incredulous look in her eyes.

"Is that why you took forever to kiss me?" she asked with a laugh.

He didn't buy it. She was struggling under the weight of what he had said. *Why, when she had known how much he had loved her?*

"I mean, I might as well have been wearing a T-shirt that said Take My Virginity that first week."

Laughter barreled out of him. "I don't remember you coming onto me that hard."

"That's not a surprise. Every woman on that cruise ship wanted a bite of the GMM. I had very stiff competition—especially from that hot dancer."

Wasn't *she* full of surprises? "What's GMM?"

A blush dusted her cheeks pink. "Glorious Man Meat."

"Aah…I'm very honored."

"Liv's term. Two minutes after meeting you I finally got what she meant." A naughty smile—a very rare sight—split her mouth. "Though now, what with you all old, out of shape and with this whole daddy-in-the-making thing—" her gaze caressed his body in a swift sweep, belying her words "—I think we can pass the title of GMM on to Miguel," she finished with a dreamy sigh.

The little cat was needling him on purpose. But it was this cheeky, smiling side of her that got to him. He leaned into her and clasped her face with his hands.

Before he could think better of it, he touched his mouth to hers.

The barest of contacts was enough to spread a wildfire of need inside him. With a groan that was torn out of him, he pulled her close and devoured the lushness of her mouth.

Her fingers dug into his arms. She mewled against his

mouth, a sound made deep in her throat that slithered over his skin.

He half dragged her into his lap, his hands spanning her thin waist, seeking and searching the curve of her breasts.

Droga, but she was all soft and warm, the stretchy fabric of her swimsuit no barrier. He closed his hands over her covered breasts, felt the tightened nipples grazing his palms. He rubbed his palms up and down and her mouth opened on a soft moan.

"*Meu Deus,* I touch you and you blow up like TNT..."

He plunged his tongue inside her mouth and licked the inseam. He felt lightheaded with desire, every drop of blood flowing south.

He pressed wet kisses down to her neck—just as the two floodlights on the opposite sides of the terrace came on, drowning them in bright light.

With a gasp, Kim slid off his lap. Her lips were swollen and pink, her hair all mussed up. Their gazes met in silence for a second, before both of them burst out laughing.

"I'm thinking that was Miguel, right?" she said, her smile still in place.

Her taste lingering on his mouth, he nodded. "Sorry."

"No, it's good he stopped us when he did. Of course I *did* earn my kiss, but you don't want to give me too many points."

He raised a brow.

A teasing glint appeared in her eyes. "Remember? Sexual points for good behavior? You kissed me because I moved in, right? Like a dutiful little wife? Or was that just you forgetting your own—?"

He made a quick lunge to catch her, but she was too fast this time. With lithe grace she moved to the other side of the lounger. Her robe half dangled around her elbows, giving him a perfect view of her swimsuit-clad body.

Holding his stomach tight, he sucked in a sharp breath. His wife was hot. There was no other word for it.

Like everything else she wore, the swimsuit was modest, a one-piece in hot pink. But it showcased the swell of her high breasts, the dip of her dainty waist…which would soon be rounded…the slight flare of her hips and long legs that went on forever. The memory of how she had wrapped them around him while he had thrust into her, her tight heat clenching him. He was rock-hard just thinking about it.

Which meant it was time to walk away, however painful the simple act was.

She tied the sash on her robe, stepping back as he reached her. He raised his hands. "Stay and have your swim," he said. "I need to have a talk with Miguel anyway."

She waylaid him again. If she kept touching him like that, one of these days he wasn't going to be able to walk away. "I forgot to ask—how is Eduardo?"

Just hearing his half brother's name felt as if someone had stuck a knife in his side. He stilled, the ball of guilt around his neck threatening to choke the life out of him. He had lived through busted kneecaps, broken bones and so much more, but this clawing, crippling guilt—it was going to gouge him alive from inside out.

"I'm surprised he's not still following you around. He worshipped you."

Every word out of her mouth was true, and every single word dug into his skin like the sharp end of a knife.

"Diego?"

He jerked back from her. "He's in a rehabilitation clinic in Sao Paulo."

"What? Why?"

Eduardo was the best kind of reminder as to how far Diego could go when he was obsessed with something— when he let something he wanted have control over him.

Then, it had been pursuit of his wealth. Now it could be the woman in front of him, waiting for an answer.

"He's receiving treatment for a cocaine addiction."

"Eduardo used cocaine? But he used to be so… That's awful. He was always so sweet and kind to me."

Kind and sweet. They were the perfect words to describe Eduardo.

Fisting his hands, Diego rocked on his heels, bile filling his throat.

His half brother had been a nice kid, weak at heart, forever bullied by the man who had fathered them—which Diego had learned too late. Diego should have protected him. Instead Diego had been the one who nudged him that last step toward his own self-destruction.

But he wouldn't give up. He would never give up on him. If Eduardo didn't have the will to fight for his life anymore Diego would fight for him. He would use every cent he had, would wield all his power, if it meant he could get his half brother back.

CHAPTER SEVEN

KIM SCRUNCHED HER eyes closed and tried to recall all the literature she had been reading over the past month. With little Jennie wailing in her arms and that image from her afternoon appointment flashing before her eyes it was all a blur. *There were two. She wasn't even equipped for one.*

Telling Laura, her company's design architect, that she would look after little Jennie for a couple of hours had seemed like a good idea. She had been reading all about how to take care of a baby for almost a month. So of course she was ready for a ground test, right?

Wrong.

Sweat beaded her brow. Her arms were starting to ache a little bit.

She bent her knees and picked up the cheat sheet she had made out of Laura's instructions, even though she knew them by heart.

She had warmed the pumped milk to precisely the exact temperature, tested it on her wrist, had fed Jennie and even tried to burp her. And then she'd put her down for a nap. Not a minute early or late.

The nap had lasted ten minutes, ending in a loud wail. According to Laura's schedule Jennie should have napped for at least an hour.

Tucking the baby tighter against her chest, she swung a little from side to side, imitating what she had seen Laura do when she had brought the baby to the company's premises a couple of times.

Her chubby cheeks scrunched up tight, Jennie wailed louder. The muscles in Kim's arms quivered until she shook all over. Even her head was beginning to pound now.

She increased the pace of her walk, tension tugging her skin tight. She should call Laura and take Jennie back to her. Every hysterical inch of her wanted to. *Will you desert your child when it gets hard?* the annoyingly logical part of her asked.

No, she couldn't accept failure—yet.

She heard the door open and turned around. Why hadn't she thought of Anna?

Diego stood in the doorway, frowning.

Her heart sank to her feet, dismay making her weak-kneed.

His gaze amused, he checked his watch.

"Was I gone *that* long?"

"You said you were going to Sao Paulo."

They both spoke at the same time.

His mouth tightened. As it did every time their conversation skated anywhere near Eduardo. "My trip got postponed."

Her shoulders felt as if there were metal rods tied to them, crushing her with their weight. The last thing she needed was for Diego to see her abysmal failure.

"What's with the baby?"

"She's—"

"Laura's. I know. She had her with her last week."

She nodded, insecurities sawing at her throat. Of course he remembered Jennie from that one visit—while Kim had always scrambled even to remember her name.

He had picked her up one evening last week from work—a strangely domestic but comforting gesture—and she had been forced to introduce her staff to him. All forty of them—from their sixty-year-old office manager Karen to nineteen-year-old intern Amy—had mooned over him. *And* informed her with a sigh the next morning that they understood her actions perfectly.

"Kim?"

She sighed. Jennie's little mewls were picking up volume again. "I offered to look after her for a few hours."

A single eyebrow shot into his hairline. "Why?"

She raised her voice to be heard over the infant's cries. "I decided to take myself on a test drive, and Laura's the only one with a baby."

"You're *practicing* because you're pregnant?"

"Something like that."

"Isn't that a little extreme?"

"I believe in being prepared."

"Prepared for what?"

She pushed her hair out of her face with her free hand, trying to ignore his gaze drilling into her.

"I...I don't know what's wrong with her. She won't calm down." Hitching Jennie up with her one hand, she wiped her forehead. "I've fed her, changed her and tried to burp her. I'm running out of ideas except to take her back."

She looked around the cozy sitting area she had taken over for the evening, taking in the untouched protein shake, the dirty diaper on the rug, Jennie's blanket trailing over the edge of the designer leather couch...

But it was the clawing urge to take Jennie back to Laura and pretend the evening had never happened that gutted her.

Tears burned in the back of her throat, gathering momentum like a storm.

Dear God, how was she...?

Diego's hard frame in front of her pulled her to a stop.

Jennie's wails were becoming incessant, her little face scrunched up tight. Kim's heart sank to the floor. She was ready to bawl her *own* eyes out.

She raised her gaze to Diego, her neck stiff, her forearms strained to the point of shaking. "She won't stop crying, Diego."

He took Jennie from her, his movements infinitely gentle. The little girl fit on his forearm with room to spare.

Kim's heart lurched into her throat.

With curious ease he held Jennie high in the cradle of his arms, her pink dress contrasting against his rough, large hands. "Might be because you're holding her too tight and she can feel your tension."

"That's not true. She was crying long before I picked her up…"

The infant immediately stopped crying, as though confirming Diego's statement. He swung the cradle of his arms left to right, gently, his gaze never moving from Jennie.

Kim froze as he cooed to her. It was the most wonderful sight she had ever seen.

"Babies are very sensitive to our own moods and personalities."

His soft words landed like a slap on her. "What the hell does *that* mean?"

The look he threw her, puzzled and doubting, pierced through the last shred of her composure.

"It means that she can sense that you're nervous—*wound up.*" His gaze drilled into her. "*Overwrought, stressed out…* do you want me to go on? What *you* feel is setting *her* off. If you just—"

"I get it—okay!" she said, practically shouting.

Every muscle in her trembled, and her chest was so tight that it was an effort to breathe. As long as it had just been in her head it had still been bearable. Given voice like that, it tore through her.

"She can sense that I don't care, that I want to be doing anything but looking after her. That's it, right?"

* * *

Diego lowered the sleeping infant into the tiny bassinet and tucked her in tight. The little girl settled in without a whisper, and he rubbed his thumb over a plump cheek.

A soft, sleepy gurgle erupted from the baby's tiny mouth.

Whatever his past sins, the new life that was coming was a precious gift. If only he could figure out what was worrying Kim.

Familiar frustration spiked through him. The past few weeks they had fallen into a somewhat torturous routine of sorts. With each passing day and every single minute they spent in each other's company—and this was with both of them avidly trying to keep it to a minimum—he had realized how hard it was to keep his hands to himself. Especially when he had begun to see glimpses of the girl he had fallen in love with so long ago.

She still hadn't cut down her work hours, but she *had* spent the last Sunday home watching a soccer game with him and Miguel. Who, interestingly, had said more to her than he had to Diego.

He might even say she was slowly letting her guard down with him. Except when Anna or he brought up the pregnancy.

Then she immediately retreated behind that shell of hers. She refused to share what was on her mind. And yet more than once he had seen her reading articles on motherhood on her tablet, lost in deep thought.

And tonight she had borrowed a baby. Because she had known he would be out for the night.

Foreboding inched across his skin. Once he had been too involved in his own world and had neglected Eduardo when he had needed him. He wasn't going to make the same mistake again. He was going to get to the root of what was bothering her tonight.

He eyed her across the room. She was plumping the

same pillow on the couch, her shoulders stiff with tension, her punches into it increasing steadily, until her jabs were vicious and accompanied by soft grunts.

He reached her quickly, meaning to catch her before she buried whatever was troubling her under grating self-sufficiency. With a hand on her shoulder, he turned her around. "If you're imagining that to be my face," he said, "let me…"

She let him look at her for only a second before she pushed away from him. But what he had seen in that second was enough to stun Diego.

Tears filled her huge brown eyes.

His breath felt as if it had been knocked out of him—as if someone had clocked his jaw. He had never seen her tears. Not when he had humiliated her, not when he had threatened her company, not even when her father had shredded her.

With an arm thrown around her waist he tugged her hard against him and locked her there. She was plastered to him from shoulder to thigh. Her soft flesh shuddered and rearranged itself against him.

"Let me go."

"Shhh…" he whispered near her ear, knowing that she was extra-sensitive to any touch there. "I just want to look at you."

Her hands against his chest, she glared at him, her tears unshed.

Every inch of her was taut, like a tightly wound spring, and a slow tremor was inching through her. Something had shaken her up badly. He tightened his arms around her, waiting for the tremors to pass.

Dark blue shadows danced under her huge eyes. Her hair was not the sleek polished silk that gleamed every time she moved her face in that arrogant, thoroughly sexy way of hers. Instead it curled around her face, lending a false vulnerability to the sharp angles of her face.

But the fact that she was close to exhaustion was written in the dull pallor of her skin, in the pinched look stamped upon her features.

His ire rose to the surface again, and he didn't fool himself that he was worried for his unborn child. The anxiety that he couldn't purge from his system, the anger that had his muscles quivering for action, was all for *her*.

Despite his best intentions he just couldn't *not* care about her.

He moved his hand up from her waist to her nape and dug his fingers into her hair, held her tight.

His grip didn't hurt her. He knew that. But he needed that hold on her for a second—the deceptive illusion of control over her, over her emotions.

Because she reduced him to what he'd been born to.

All the trappings of wealth, all the polish he had acquired in the past six years, fell away, reducing him to what he was at his core. Someone who had been born into the gutter and craved a better life that had remained out of his grasp for so long.

There was always a part of her that remained unreachable, unattainable to him, as though he still didn't make the cut.

He trailed his gaze over her, from the well-worn Harvard T-shirt that hugged her breasts to the low slung sweatpants that left a strip of flesh bare at her midriff.

"You can't stop shivering. You look awful," he said.

Pushing away from him, she glanced down over herself. Distaste marred her brow. "I spent last night at work and I didn't have time for a shower when I came back."

"Aren't you working enough without taking on baby-sitting?"

She glanced at Jennie and trembled again. "I just… I

wanted to see if I could handle her for a few hours." The resigned curve of her mouth tugged at him.

"*Meu Deus,* what is the matter with you?"

Silence.

He frowned, resisting the urge to shake her by her shoulders. He had never seen her so defeated, never heard that self-deprecating tone in her words. He picked her up and settled down into the recliner with her in his lap. The fact that she sagged into him without a protest alarmed the hell out of him.

"You look like you're ready to tip over. Answer my question, *pequena.* What's going on?"

She tucked her knees in closer. Tears rolled over her cheeks. "There are two, Diego."

He raked his mind. "Two... *Two what, gatinha?*"

"Two heartbeats."

He pushed her chin up none too gently. *"What?"*

A shadow descended on her face, her skin a tight mask over the fine bones. "I went to see the doctor today for a routine checkup. She thought it best to do an ultrasound. There are two... Diego, there are twins."

His mouth slack, Diego couldn't believe her words. Incredible joy flushed through him. He was going to be a father to not one but two babies. He had no breath left in him. He felt lightheaded, as if nothing could mar his happiness anymore. He was going to have a family—a proper one—with *two* babies looking to him for everything.

He shivered at the magnitude of what it meant.

It had been a shock when he had first learned of the baby, but now all he felt was exceptionally blessed. As if for the first time in as far as he could remember he had a chance to be something good, to build something good—as if life had finally handed him a good turn.

Gathering Kim tight in his arms, he pressed a kiss to her upturned mouth and tasted her tears.

He pulled back from her, the worry etched into her pinched mouth, the sheer terror in her gaze, puncturing his own joy.

"That's why you brought Jennie over? Why you're practicing?"

He cupped her jaw, forcing her to look at him. His mouth felt dry. Words were hitching in his throat. He palmed her back, up and down, looking for words to do this right.

Because he had never been in this position of offering comfort or strength to her—ever. She had never leaned on him for anything. Her unwavering strength was both incredibly amazing and annoying at the same time.

"This is not something where we practice for perfection, *gatinha*," he said softly, anxious to remove anything negative from his words. "We just try to do our best."

"But that's not enough, is it? Good intentions and effort can't make up for what's missing. You told me once your mother had never been able to scrape enough money to feed you properly, but you didn't care, did you? Because you knew that she loved you."

"As will you love our children. I told you before—we don't have to be perfect parents; we just have to love them enough—"

She fought against his grip again, a whimper escaping her. That pained sound sent a shiver racing up his spine.

"Whatever is paining you, I swear I will help you through it, *gatinha*. Tell me, what is—?"

"I'm not good with babies." Her words sounded as if they were tortured, as if they were ripped from her. "I'll never be, so it's a good thing you're here. Or else our kids might never stop crying—might turn out just like me, hating their mother."

Something squeezed in his chest and he released a hard breath, shoving aside his own conflicted emotions for the minute.

"And the fact that you're exhausted has nothing to do with it?"

She bit her lip. Her uncertainty—something he had never seen—was a shock to his system.

"How do you feel about being a full-time stay-at-home daddy?"

He smiled even as stark fear gripped him. "And what will *you* do?"

"I'll do everything else." She ran her tongue over her lips, her brow tied into that line that it got when she was in full-on thinking mode. "I'll work, I'll clean, I'll cook. I'll even—" She stopped, as though she had just caught on to the desperation in her words. Her tears spilled over from her eyes, her slender shoulders trembling under the weight of perplexing grief. "I don't feel anything, Diego."

His heart stopped for a minute, if that was possible. "What does that mean?"

"For the babies. I don't feel *anything*."

He sucked in a breath, the anguish he spied in her gaze sending waves of powerlessness hurling through him.

"Except this relentless void, there's nothing inside of me when I think of them," she said, rushing over her words as though she couldn't stop them anymore. "I should look forward to it now, at least. I should be used to it by now. At first I thought it was because I was angry with you. Because you were the father. It's not. *It is me.* All I can think is how I wish it was anyone but me. *Every waking moment.* I can't bear to look at myself because I'm afraid I will see changes I don't want to. My team is more excited about this than I am. The ultrasound technician was more excited than I was when we looked at them. *And now there are two.* What if I never feel anything for them? What if all these years of…? What if I never love them? They'll realize that, won't they? God, I would just curl up and die if they—"

"Shh…" Diego swallowed past the tears sawing at his throat and hugged her tight, pouring everything he couldn't say into the embrace. He couldn't bear to see her like this. This pain—her pain—it hammered at him with the quiet efficiency of a hundred blows.

How blithely had he assumed she didn't give a damn about anything but herself? How easily had he let her rejection of him color everything else? How easily had he let his own hangups blind him to her pain?

Her cutting indifference every time she had mentioned the pregnancy had been the perfect cover for this terrifying panic beneath. Regret skewered through him.

He pressed his mouth to her temple and breathed her scent in. He had no idea if it was for his or her benefit. "You built a million-dollar company from nothing but your talent and your hard work. Don't tell me your failure with Jennie tonight means you won't love our children."

Her upper body bowed forward, her forehead coming to rest on his shoulder as though the fight was literally deflating her. "I've spent years cauterizing myself against feeling anything. I think I did it so well that nothing can reach me now."

"That's nonsense." Diego wrapped his hands around her and tucked her closer to him. "You care about your sister. You told me you tried your best to protect her from your father's wrath. I'm sure once the babies come you—"

"I'm the reason Liv suffered so much at my dad's hands. It was my responsibility to protect her. Nothing else."

"What are you talking about?"

"You think you're the only one who has a monopoly on guilt?"

Frustration boiled through Diego as defiance crept back into her tone. Her shields fell back into place, the pain shoved away beneath layers and layers of indifference. His hold over her was just as fleeting as always.

* * *

Feeling Diego stiffen against her, Kim slid out of his reach. Her knees threatened to collapse under her, but anything was better than the cocoon of his embrace.

It had felt so good. The temptation to buy into his words that everything would be fine, the need to dump the bitterest truth in his lap, had been dangerous.

Except she was sure there would be nothing but distaste left on his face if she did that. She would take his anger anytime.

That was what living with him was doing to her—slowly but surely eroding everything she had learned to survive.

"How come you're so good at it?" she threw at him, the pain dulling to a slow ache.

For now there was nothing to do but wait. That was the part that was slowly driving her crazy. There wasn't a way to *make* herself feel. There was no switch to turn it on.

"I'm not. But Marissa always has a baby attached to her hip, and I think I've picked up a thing or two in all these years."

An image of a laughing, petite brunette flashed in front of Kim's eyes. Her mouth burned with the acidic taste of jealousy. Until now she had held on, pretended even to herself that he didn't matter to her, that falling into his bed four weeks ago had been nothing but a mistake.

"Marissa?"

He nodded slowly, a flat, hardened look replacing the tenderness she had seen seconds ago, as though he resented Kim even uttering her name. Not as though. *He hated it.* It was there in the way his stance stiffened, in the way he turned away from her.

"You were…?" Kim swallowed, forcing the lump in her throat down, that acidic taste burning her mouth. "You've been with *her* all these—?"

He shrugged. "Over the years Marissa and I have always

drifted toward each other. In between deserting spouses, deaths and even…" His gaze fell to Jennie and his mouth curved into a little smile. "She's nothing if not maternal."

The last sentence was like driving a knife into her already torn-up gut. "But you're not with her anymore because of me?"

His gaze collided with her. "Because you're pregnant with my child."

Kim flinched.

"When I learned of your wedding I was furious. Marissa didn't like my reaction. She gave me an ultimatum. I had to finish things with you if I wanted a life with her."

"But that means you…" She blinked. "You didn't come to the island to sed…to sleep with me?" She corrected herself at the last minute.

The arrogant resolve in his eyes dissolved and she sucked in a sharp breath.

"No. I wanted to see you one last time, to show you what I had become. To throw the divorce papers in your face and walk away. Instead I saw you and lost my mind again."

Bitter disappointment knuckled her in the gut. How pathetic was it that she felt cheated because Diego hadn't come to find her for some elaborate revenge scheme? That she hadn't merited even that much of his energy?

Exactly as she hadn't with her own mother.

She bit out a laugh. It was either that or dissolve into tears. "And I fell pregnant and ruined your plans…and hers."

He shot up from the couch and materialized in front of her. "It would be so much easier if I could blame you, but we were both there."

"Oh *please*. Will you stop with the whole honorable act? I would much prefer seeing the hatred in your eyes than looking for things that are not there."

"*I* hurt her, Kim. Not you. The one thing she asked of me was to finish things with you. Because of my insane obsession with you, because of my refusal to leave you alone—" every word out of his mouth reverberated with bitter disgust, and the depth of it slammed into her "—I...I broke her heart, and there's no way to fix it. I have to live with that guilt my entire life."

He stepped away from her as though he couldn't bear to be near her now Marissa had been mentioned, as though even looking at her compounded his guilt.

"I'll send Anna down. She will look after Jennie," he said, halting with his hand on the doorhandle. "Make sure you eat something and get some sleep. Think of the babies, if nothing else."

She sank to the couch as he closed the door behind him. She had hated him for setting her up, for ruthlessly walking away, but he had paid the price for their reckless passion just as she had.

She wished with every cell in her being that he was the ruthless man she had thought him. Because the man he was underneath—kind and thoughtful—how was she supposed to resist him?

He could have thrown her ineptitude in her face, laughed at her fears. Wasn't that why she had been stewing in it by herself? But he hadn't.

He had held her, hugged her, tried to make her feel better. He had been genuinely concerned for her. He could make it so easy for her to depend on him, to bask in his concern, to fall deeper and deeper...

That was if she wasn't *already* in exactly the situation she had fought so hard against.

Her legs shook as she hugged herself. She needed Diego in her life. No, she *wanted* Diego in her life. But the gnawing, terrifying truth was that nothing but his honor was keeping him there.

Nothing about *her* was keeping him there.

CHAPTER EIGHT

IT WAS, WITHOUT doubt, a sex party.

Diego had no other name for it. His thoughts had swung from mild curiosity to full-blown agitation when a six-foot bouncer had checked his ID at the entrance and announced that admittance cost ten thousand dollars.

He had spent the better part of the evening trying to find Kim. It was half past ten now, and this was where her colleague had finally directed him to.

The party was in full swing in a two-floor Manhattan loft that had taken him several phone calls to locate. He scowled and moved past a waitress dressed in a French maid's costume serving hors d'oeuvres.

Soft, sultry music streamed through the richly carpeted foyer from cleverly hidden sub-woofers. Pink neon lights strategically placed on the low ceiling bathed the lounge, illuminating the retro-style furniture and a bar. It was very elegantly done, with a high-class Parisian feel to it.

The lower floor was dotted with futons against the retro chic walls, and in the corner a thin, exotically dressed woman was working massage oil into a naked man's back. On the other side of the full bar was a huge dance floor, where at least twenty men and women were softly bumping into one another.

He gritted his teeth and loosened his tie. What the hell was Kim doing *here?* Was this to compensate for the vulnerability she hadn't been able to hide yesterday? Or was it an act of defiance to rile him up because he had organized her day today?

He glanced up the curving staircase toward the more expansive upper floor. Every muscle in him tightened as his gaze fell on more than one couple getting hot and heavy up there, their moans adding to the soulful music downstairs.

A sudden chill hit Diego. Which floor was Kim on?

Running a hand over his nape, he moved toward the dimly lit lounge. He had no idea what he would do if he didn't find her on the lower floor. Already every base instinct in him was riled up at the very fact that she was here, of all places.

If he found her with... No, that thought didn't even bear thinking.

He reached the outer edge of the dance floor, searching for her. He froze at the edge of the crowd as he finally located her. She was right in the center of the crowd, her hands behind her head, moving in perfect rhythm to the music, while a smartly dressed man had his hands around her waist.

His blood roared in his veins. *Mine,* the barely civilized part in him growled.

She was only dancing, he reminded himself, before he gave in to the urge to beat the crap out of the man touching her. A caveman—just as she had called him.

He slowly walked the perimeter of the crowd.

Her eyes closed, her legs bent, she was moving with an irresistible combination of grace and sensuality that lit a fire in his blood. Every muscle in his body tightened with a razor-edged hunger.

Her hair shone like raw silk. Her mouth was painted a vivid dark red, almost black, like nothing he'd ever seen on her before. Usually her lips shimmered with the barest gloss. A black leather dress hugged every inch of her—

cupping her breasts high, barely covering her buttocks. The dress left her shoulders bare, and the exposed curves of her breasts were the sexiest sight he had ever seen.

She'd done the rest of her face differently, too, heavier make-up than he had ever seen. Usually the lack of make-up only served to heighten the no-nonsense, made-of-ice vibe she projected.

It was the opposite today—that outfit, her make-up, everything signaled sexual availability, grabbing attention and keeping it there. Was that why she was here? What had prompted this out-of-character interest in a sex party, of all things?

She looked like his darkest fantasy come true.

Lust knuckled him in the gut. All he wanted to do was pull the dress down until her breasts fell into his hands, past her hips until she was laid bare for him, and then plunge into her until neither of them could catch their breath, until the roar in his blood stopped.

He moved closer to her without blinking, his heart pounding in his ribcage, his skin thrumming with need. Her gaze lit upon him and shock flashed in it. Good—she'd recognized him.

He stepped on the raised platform and roughly collared the guy dancing with her, moved him out of the way. He palmed her face and tilted it up roughly. "Are you high?"

"What?" Even her question sounded uneven. "Of course not."

He sniffed her. Nothing but the erotic scent of her skin met his nostrils. His jeans felt incredibly tight. It was all he could do to stop from pressing into her. If he did, he didn't think he could stop. "Are you drunk?" he said, noting a hoarse note in his own words.

She shook her head, something dangerous inching into her gaze. She ran a hand over her midriff, drawing Diego's gaze to the dress again. "If you're just going to spoil my fun…"

He blocked her as she turned away from him, the forward momentum pushing her breasts to graze against his chest. He clamped his fingers around her arm and tugged her.

She turned to face him. A strip of light illuminated the lush curve of her mouth, leaving the rest of her face in shadow. "What are you doing?"

He bent his head and tugged her lip with his teeth. Molten heat exploded in every nerve. His cock ached hard. Her hissing breath felt like music to his ears. "Taking you home."

She dug her heels in and he loosened his hold. "I'm not ready to leave yet."

"Yes, you are."

To hell with all his rules, and with sanity and with whatever crap he had spun to keep things rational between them.

She was *his*—whether she knew it or not, whether she liked it or not. And not just because she was going to be the mother of his children.

Kim pulled the flaps of Diego's leather jacket tighter around her and stepped out of the limo. A gust of wind barreled into her. She folded her hands against her midriff, her mouth falling open as she realized why the drive from the party had taken so long. Diego had been talking non-stop on his cell phone, effectively silencing any questions she had.

They were at a private airstrip. The ground crew was finishing up its prep, and the aircraft was being revved up. A tremor traveled up and down her spine.

She walked toward Diego, who was still talking on his phone.

His gaze traveled the length of her once again, intractable.

"What's going on?"

He clicked his phone shut. "I have something urgent to take care of."

Her stomach tightened. "So go. I'll even bid you goodbye with a smile."

"You're coming with me. You can laze in a spa, swim in a beach, shop for maternity clothes…among other things."

Her skin sizzled at the double intonation on the last bit.

"Everything you *should* be doing."

Her breath hitched in her throat at the resolve in his gaze. "You like lording it over me, don't you? I'm not going anywhere with you."

He took a step toward her and backed her against the limo. He pulled her hand into his and twined their fingers. She felt his touch to the tip of her toes.

"I was worried about you. I am still. So shut up and accept it."

Her heart thumped inside her ribcage. Gooey warmth flooded through her. No one had ever worried about her. *Ever.* It had been her job to worry for as long as she could remember.

She had worried about her mom first, shielded her from her father. And after she had walked out she had tried her best to protect Liv from her dad's wrath. No one had ever seen past the veneer of her perfection to the emptiness beneath—even Liv, who cared about her….

With his thumb and forefinger he rubbed over her forehead. "Stop thinking so much. You will stay with me so that I can keep an eye on you."

"Why?"

"You didn't seem yourself last night. Or just now."

"Last night I was hormonal. Tonight I'm horny."

Liquid fire blazed in his gaze.

"Those are the only colors on my rainbow lately."

He laughed, the sexy dimple in his cheek winking at her.

"Hormonal and horny women *need* looking after."

It had been a very strange day on so many accounts.

Once the janitor had locked her out of her company's premises she had returned to her apartment, fuming with disbelief. Because for the past six years she had worked every Saturday except the day she had gone to her wedding.

By the time she had finished every last scrap of the delicious sandwich Anna had given her, taking away her laptop in the process, and with her usual intelligence deserting her, Kim had realized too late that everything had been orchestrated by Diego.

Total lack of sleep last night meant she had zonked out for the rest of the day.

"I came to check on you twice and you were sleeping. Anyone with a little sense can see your body needs rest. Why do I have to force you to it?"

She flushed, unbidden warmth spurting in her. He had checked on her. *Twice.* She should resent his high-handed attitude; she should at least offer token resistance. But she couldn't muster a protest past the warm fuzzies filling her up.

When had anyone ever checked on her? This was the same strangely weakening, cared-for sensation that had driven her to marry him six years ago. She had stupidly wanted that feeling to last forever.

"And what were you doing *there,* of all places?"

He sounded so aggravated that she smiled. "I was going crazy after sleeping straight through the day. So I made a list of all the things I need to get ready before the babies come. Then I—"

He tapped her temple with one long finger. "I'm going to cure you of your overthinking if it's the last thing I do."

"Then I got thinking of all the things I won't get to do anymore *when* the babies arrive."

"And going to a sex club was one of them?" His frown deepened into a full-fledged scowl. "What else was on it?"

The flare of interest in his gaze goaded her. Last night had been terrifying on so many levels. Right at that moment she would do anything to see what he felt for her reflected there. Even if it was just lust.

"Sex with a stranger was number two and sex in a public place number three. I thought I could shoot two birds with one—"

He tilted forward, all two hundred pounds of hulking, turned-on, prime male focused on her. A tingle started deep in her lower back and began inching its way all over. Her palms slapped onto his chest as he angled his lower body closer.

"You're pushing me on purpose, *pequena*. Are you ready for the consequences?"

His rock-hard thigh lodged in between her thighs, sparking an ache in that exact spot. A whimper clawing out of her, she pushed at him. The feel of hard muscles and the thundering of his heart under her fingers was just as torturous.

The heat uncoiling in his gaze made mincemeat of her. "Okay, fine. I made that up," she said, cupping his jaw. "I…I didn't know what to do with myself. But if you're going to rearrange my everyday life the least you can do is…"

His gaze locked on her mouth and he relented the pressure of his thigh just a little. "What?"

"Let me enjoy it the way I want to."

"Coward."

A slow smile—one that should come with a health warning—curved his mouth, digging deep grooves into his face. Glorious warmth unraveled inside her. She loved it when he looked at her like that, when he smiled like that. As if she was the only one in the world who could put it there.

It was wishful thinking at best, dangerous indulgence at worst, but she couldn't fight the feeling.

"It kills you to ask, doesn't it? To admit, even if only for a second, you wanted to see me?"

She smiled, incapable of resisting him at that moment. "I did call your secretary. She had no idea when you would be back. So I took Carla's offer."

"The sex expert on your team? Carla was there too?"

She smacked his chest with the back of her hand at the exaggerated interest in his words.

A car pulled up alongside their limo, the headlights illuminating the airstrip.

Miguel stepped out of the dark sedan. He opened the trunk and pulled out a pretty pink suitcase which, even in the low light, looked familiar.

Her jaw hit her chest. "That's mine."

"I had Anna pack some of your things." He nodded at Miguel, who disappeared back into the car without a word to Kim. "Let's go."

He was serious. He was taking her away on a holiday. She shouldn't be so happy about it, but she was. "But I—"

"You're taking a few days off. Do you want to spend it alone? Maybe interview some more nannies? Borrow another baby? Dodge more calls from Olivia?"

Heat tightened her cheeks. She was getting more than a little obsessive in her *Planning for Pregnancy* phase. As if she could somehow make up for lacking the most necessary part of it. And, judging by the way Diego was looking at her, he knew that she was slowly going insane.

For the first time in her life she didn't want to be alone. She didn't have any strength left.

"I can't just leave like that, Diego. I run a company. My laptop—"

He turned around. "It's in there," he said, with a nod toward another bag she hadn't noticed before.

Her laptop case. She hated it when anyone touched it. Her most precious possession was in there.

She moved to take it from him but he held it behind him.

"I'm warning you again. This is a vacation. Mary and Amber have already been informed."

Her assistant and her VP of Operations.

"I will send this back with Miguel unless you agree that your time on it will be limited."

"*Limited?* What does that mean?" she said, hurrying behind him.

He paused at the foot of the plane's stairs, one hand extended toward her. "You'll be allowed one hour every day on that laptop."

Reaching him, she paused. "What am I supposed to do for the rest of the day?"

His hand clasping hers, he smiled, the very devil lurking in his gaze. "I'm sure we will find something enjoyable."

She waited until they were settled into the flight and she had picked at her dinner before she started looking around her seat.

Without asking, Diego knew what she was looking for. He couldn't believe it. The woman really was a workaholic.

"Where's my laptop case?" she threw at him, meeting his gaze.

"It should be somewhere here." Her expression anxious, she unbuckled her seat belt and stood up.

He leaned forward and grabbed her hand, stopping her. "This is what I'm talking about. What is so important that you need it *now?*"

With her other hand she pushed at his hold. "I don't." She looked almost panicky. "I just… I want to make sure it doesn't get misplaced."

He stared at her for a few seconds before replying, "It's in the rear cabin."

After a few minutes he followed her there, unable to keep his mind on anything else.

She knelt by the small side table next to the bed and unzipped the case. Smiling, he hunkered down on his knees next to her.

"What are you looking for?"

Her gaze wide, she froze with her hand inside the case. "Oh, just a…an old CD of songs I made a while ago. I want to upload it to my iPod and I…" She swallowed as he didn't budge. "I would prefer to do it alone."

He laughed. "Send me on my way so that you can work? *No.*"

"Never mind." She began zipping it closed. "I don't think the CD's in here anyway."

He grabbed the leather case from her.

Her hand shaking, she tugged it back. "No, Diego… Don't…"

"You are acting *really* strange," he murmured, and tugged the zipper open.

A bulging envelope fell out—a faded one, with a logo he instantly recognized. It was from a photo studio in Rio where he'd used to have his pictures developed long ago.

Where she had gone to have the pictures developed from the disposable cameras she and Eduardo had carried on that cruise.

She grabbed it and tucked her hand behind her jerkily.

He met her gaze, his chest incredibly tight. The last thing he wanted was to remember the pain he had felt when she had walked out. Not when they were finally starting over again, even if not with a clean slate.

The memory brushed his words with a harsh edge. "I'm surprised you didn't burn them all a long time ago."

Hurt flashed in her gaze. Still on her haunches, she moved away from him, as though she was shielding a precious commodity. "They're catalogued under 'Mistakes Never to Be Repeated.'"

"Why do you have them in your laptop case?"

Her answer was extremely reluctant. "When I packed my stuff to be moved I put them in there, to keep at work."

So that he didn't see them even by accident.

Anger burning through him, he made a quick move. The envelope fell from her arms, scattering pictures all around him. Every one of them showed Kim and him, happy, smiling, the world around them faded to nothing.

He grabbed a couple and crumpled them in his hand.

She gasped and plucked at his hand, her fingers digging into his bunched fist. "No... What are you doing?"

"I'm going to do what you should have done—tear them and trash them."

She was trembling. "Don't you dare."

He grabbed another one, seething inside. He was about to rip it in half, when she clamped his wrist, her grip strong as a vise.

She shook her head, hot anger burning in her eyes. "Stop it, Diego."

He let the picture go and pulled her toward him. "Why did you leave?"

"What?"

"It's a question I should have asked years ago."

"Believe me, the answer won't make you happy."

With a grunt, she tried to pry his fingers open. Her nails, even though blunt, dug into his knuckles. He didn't care, and apparently neither did she.

"Let it go, Diego."

"No. Not unless you answer my question. And truth this time."

"I've never lied to you."

"You've never told me the truth either. Like the fact that you never slept with Alexander."

Her gaze flashed to him even while her fingers still jabbed at his. "Is that it? You want to know how many men I've slept with in my life? Two—you first, and then this other guy a year after I left you, because I couldn't forget you. But it was horrible. There—are you happy?"

A red haze descended in front of his eyes. "What is supposed to make me happy? The fact that you would do anything to wipe me from your mind? Everything you give me—whether your word, or your promise, or even a damn kiss—I have to fight you for it. But you know what? I've fought for everything in my life and I fight dirty. So, unless you want me to rip up every picture I see here..."

Her efforts doubled. She scooted closer to him on her knees, stretched to her full height and then tilted her head to see the picture he was holding. "God, Diego, don't you dare—"

He pulled away from her and raised his hand, looked at the picture, too.

His stomach churned with a vicious force.

This one had been taken the night after he'd had sex... no, had made love to her. However much he tried, it was a night he couldn't cheapen. Not even in his thoughts.

Did she feel the same? Was that why the picture was so important to her? He was sick and tired of second-guessing.

He held it with both his hands. There was a small tear in the picture already.

She slammed into him as she tried to reach it. "Give it back, Diego..."

"No."

"Fine."

She didn't shout. And yet her words vibrated with raw pain and utter desolation.

"I left because you turned me into a prize to parade before your father—into some trophy that was a victory over your childhood."

"You said I treated you like a princess."

"Yes—a princess dressed up in glittery clothes and exhibited for the status she provided. Anyone who asked, you recited my accomplishments as though it was my résumé. You were obsessed with taking over your father's company. You spent every waking minute devising ways to get more access, more information. I…I loved you, and you broke my heart."

"How is that possible? I was ready to move so that you could go to Harvard. I wanted to give you everything you had before I—"

"I didn't want money or a grand life. I didn't want to go back to Harvard. I wanted to stay with you."

Diego's head swam with each word she uttered. "What?"

"I tried to tell you that last week. All I cared about was being with you. You didn't spend a single minute with me. We spent every evening at some gala or charity event. During the day you disappeared to God knows where. You made all these plans for how we would live our lives in New York….I didn't want that life. When I met you I was running away from that life. Liv was gone and I felt so utterly alone. I went on that cruise on an impulse and I met you. No one's ever looked at me like you did that fortnight, like there was something to me beyond… But in the end, you were the same as anyone else."

Diego forced himself to breathe past the heaviness in his throat. She clamped his wrist again, but her grip was slippery, her fingers shaking. She breathed in slowly, softly, as though it took a lot of effort.

"That picture…" Her words were low, heavy, desolate. "It represents the happiest time of my life, Diego. The only happy time. So, *please,* give it back."

His heart crawling into his throat, Diego dropped the picture. She picked it up from the floor, and the others with it, and tucked them back into the envelope hurriedly, as though she didn't trust his temper.

He had done everything she had blamed him for and more. He had come to his own conclusions about why she had left him, let it fester inside. He had let his own insecurities color her actions. He had destroyed his happiness with his own hands...

All in pursuit of the very wealth and status that had robbed him of the two people who had truly loved him, who had cared about him.

He lifted her chin, his hands shaking with impotent rage. That familiar guilt clawed through him. Another person he'd hurt, another black mark on the increasing roster of his sins.

He palmed her cheek, tracing the jutting angles of her cheekbones with his fingers. Words rushed out of him on a wave of powerlessness that pricked his muscles.

"I did love you. I couldn't bear the thought of not seeing you again once we were off that ship. That's why I married you. I...I was obsessed with defeating my father, yes, but I never meant to hurt you. But of course neither of us had enough faith in the other, did we? You didn't have enough to tell me the truth, and I didn't have enough to drag you back to me."

"Why didn't you?"

Fury such as he had never heard, rattled in her words. But she didn't wait for his answer.

He should have gone after her. But he had been able to see nothing past what he had termed as her rejection of him. He had driven himself to new, ruthless heights, manipulated and eventually driven Eduardo over the cliff.

All because she had made him realize the bitter truth that he had shoved beneath his fight for survival—that he would never be enough.

CHAPTER NINE

KIM STEPPED OUT of the shower stall in the luxurious rear cabin. She loved the circular space with its vanity lighting, but the hot water hadn't helped.

Tugging on satin shorts and a matching silk top, she put her robe back on and tied the sash. She eyed the huge bed anxiously. She trailed her fingers over the soft Egyptian cotton.

Were they going to share a bed when they couldn't even bear to look at each other?

She put a trembling hand to her forehead. Her racing thoughts were giving her a dull ache. The only time someone had put her first and she had run away from it. She wanted to go out and... What? Apologize for being a coward who had ruined their lives?

Her cell phone chirped an alarm. It was time for her multi-vitamin. She pushed at the strange sparkly bag that sat on top of her handbag with a little grunt. The bag slipped, its contents slipping onto the lush carpet at her feet. It was the goody bag from the sex party earlier that night.

She stared, aghast, at the tasteful assortment of favors scattered against the elegant rug.

Pink fur handcuffs, what were surely painful nipple clamps, two bottles of strawberry and chocolate-flavored massage oil, a contraption in shocking pink made in the shape of a...

It was a vibrator.

A sound—a cross between a gasp and a moan—escaped her. Heat pumped to her cheeks. Excitement dried her mouth. She stared at the doorway, a wild idea taking root in her.

She had had enough of his stupid rewards system. She was going to go for the jackpot.

She picked up the vibrator and settled on to a small settee facing away from the entrance to the main cabin. The smooth silicone was soft and yet hard in her hand. Sucking in a quick breath, she clicked the small button on the side.

A soft whir filled the cabin.

She didn't know what drove her to it. Maybe it was the horny part of her that she had no control over. Maybe it was the self-loathing running through her veins because she was still a coward who, instead of walking up to Diego and kissing him, as every cell in her wanted to, only dared to sit in here and play sexual peekaboo with him.

She didn't care.

She leaned against the wall, tugged her robe open and pushed it back over her shoulders.

Her PJs were nothing to write a Victoria's Secret catalog about, but at least the spaghetti strap top and the shorts were satin, in a cute shade of peach with little bows. They were not dull or boring, as Diego had said.

Her shorts exposed her legs which, thanks to Carla, she had gotten waxed for the party. Her toenails, painted the same sexy pink as the vibrator, gleamed against the cream leather couch.

The grooved velvet handle offered a sturdy grip as she held the vibrating head of it against her smooth calf. It tickled her skin and a giggle escaped her.

Laughing, she dragged the vibrating head upward from her calf. The thump-thump of her heart as she heard movement in the main cabin gobbled up the calming whir of the device.

She stalled as she reached her knee and pulled it back down. Up and down she moved it, covering a little more ground on the way up every time.

A tingle started sweeping up the base of her neck, across her face, spreading all over her skin. A shocking wetness dampened her panties. Even her palm felt slippery on the handle.

Her mouth dried up.

Because her clammy palm had nothing to do with what the device in her hand was doing to her body and everything to do with the thundering presence of the man looming at the entrance to the cabin, looking down at her from behind.

She could feel his gaze on her, daring her to raise her head and meet his gaze.

She could feel his hardened breathing in the way oxygen was swiftly depleted around her.

She could feel his arousal in the way her body reacted to his presence, in the way it was feeding off the desire he was emanating, even if she couldn't hear it or see it.

Her heart hammered. Her legs shook. Every muscle in her body trembled with an almost feverish chill. It was a good thing she had sat on the couch or she would have melted into a puddle of longing at his feet.

Bending her head, she moved the vibrating tip up past her knee this time. Her already sensitized skin vibrated with a thrumming awareness.

She reached the halfway point up her thigh.

He didn't interrupt her.

She let her boneless right leg collapse to the side, opening up her inner thigh to her hand. Her breathing quickened, the scent of arousal filling the scant air in the cabin.

He didn't make a sound.

The vibrating head reached the sensitive skin of her inner thigh. Heat crept along every inch of her skin as she moved the head a little more. Heat pooled at her sex.

He didn't move in his stance.

Her boldness had a shelf life of a few minutes at best, and it was fast running out. Sitting there, open in front of him, even with her shorts covering her aching flesh, she felt the most erotic thrill begin in her lower belly.

Over the past few seconds this had morphed into a battle of wills. He was calling her bluff, daring her to continue. And she was damned if she'd give in. She wanted his hands on her body, his fingers on her aching flesh, and she would settle for nothing less.

Refusing to look up, she moved her wrist another inch, up under the hem of her shorts. It was nowhere near where she wanted it.

She threw her head back, closed her eyes and imagined it to be his long fingers crawling up her thigh, propelling her toward ecstasy. A moan began inching its way up all the way from her lower back and she let it out.

The sound was erotic, thrilling to her own ears.

Rough hands seized the vibrator from her boneless fingers. Her eyes fell open, her body whimpering with unfulfilled desire.

His golden gaze glittering dark with fire, he loomed over her, color bleeding into his cheeks.

The desire uncoiling in his gaze was enough to scare her back into her shell—where it was safe, where she didn't risk anything.

No.

A muscle jumped in his jaw as he flipped off the vibrator and threw it across the cabin. It landed with a thud.

She pulled herself to a kneeling position. The robe slid from her arms. "You better have a good reason for throwing that away."

Tension smoldered around them, tightening every muscle in her into a quivering mass of anticipation.

"What the hell do you think you're doing?" His accent was thickened, his words rolling over each other.

She ran a hand over her throat. His gaze followed the movement hungrily. "With the *blast from the past* episode we've just had, I figured it would be forever before you wanted to touch me again, so I was taking matters—"

He pulled her flush against him, until her breasts were crushed against the solid musculature of his chest. It was heaven. It was hell. It was everything she wanted with crystal-clear clarity.

"Do you want me to touch you?"

"Yes." She dragged his hand to her chest, her heart racing. Her breasts cried out for his touch. "Here." She dragged it down to her stomach. "And here." She pulled it farther down to the juncture of her thighs. "Everywhere. Nothing but your touch will erase this pain—"

He plundered her mouth with his, swallowing her words. His lips were hard against her, grinding into her with savage need, forcing her to open up to him.

With a moan that never left her throat she gripped his shoulders and opened her mouth. He plunged his tongue into her—fast, ardent strokes that sent arrows of need shooting lower.

Molten desire pooled between her legs and she tried to squeeze them closer.

But his thigh was lodged between hers. And, God, he was so deliciously hard. She rubbed against his rock-hard muscles, groaning, whimpering.

She wanted him so much, needed him so much, and she was going to let him fill her inside out, fill every inch of her, with him, with his scent, with his touch, until the regrets gouging holes inside her were gone.

Because she wanted another chance at this. She wanted another chance with Diego.

Diego had never felt such all-consuming desire as he did for this woman. Need prickled along his skin, making his erection an instrument in self-torture. Seeing her with that blasted vibrator in her hand, her legs open in sinful invitation, was enough to push him to the edge of his control.

And he had never had much to begin with. Not when it came to her.

He plunged his tongue into her mouth with all the finesse of an impatient teenager. He licked the inseam, nipped at the sensitive flesh.

There was no tentativeness in her either. In fact the bold strokes of her tongue against his own had him thrusting his hips into her soft stomach like a randy animal.

Meu Deus, she tasted like sunshine and strawberries and the decadent promise of wild, hot sex. A hint of lily of the valley clung to her skin and filled his nostrils.

A loud whimper emanated from her when he sucked on her tongue. Her hands crawled up his nape into his hair. When she tugged his lower lip between her teeth he shuddered violently, jerking his lower body into hers.

The groove of her legs cradled his erection perfectly as she rubbed herself against him. Heat gathered low at the base of his back, balling up into unbearable need in his shaft.

How could anything that felt so good be bad?

He wanted to take her right there. Because she was his and she wanted him, and it was the one place where there was only truth between them.

He slipped his hands under the flimsy satin of her top. Her skin, silky soft and warm to the touch, slithered like velvet under his rough palms. Her breathing was harsh; her soft gasps and groans were goading him on.

He was about to tug the silky strap off her shoulder when she shook her head and pulled back.

He growled instantly, like a wild animal denied its prey at the last moment.

The next minute her hands were on the fly of his jeans. He groaned—more of a request this time than a demand—as she undid the button.

His teeth were on edge as his jeans gave in. And she wrapped her long fingers around his shaft.

With a guttural groan, he pushed into her hand, blood roaring in his veins.

His eyes flicked open when her hand stopped its mind-bending caresses.

Sweat gleaming on her brow, she was trying to tug her shorts down, but her fingers kept slipping on the satin hem. She tugged a little more and the sight of black panties peeking out from under the hemline sent his blood pressure skyrocketing.

Every inch of his body was coiled tight, anticipating the pleasure, remembering how tight and wet and good she had felt around him the last time. She tugged her top off and lust blinded him.

But it was the sight of her stomach that cleared his vision. She wasn't showing much yet, but her midriff wasn't flat either. And it stopped him in his tracks.

He didn't want to force her against the wall and be done in a minute, which he was very close to doing. This could not be about slaking his lust. He didn't want to lose control as he had done the last time. Not now. Not ever again.

Because once they did this he wouldn't stop with tonight. He wanted her in his bed for the rest of their lives. If he kept control of his sanity, if he held himself back, maybe there was hope for a civilized relationship with her after all. That was what it had to be, for the sake of his children.

He wanted *her* to lose control, he wanted *her* mindless

with pleasure and he wanted her begging for release. This time he wanted to savor every inch of her, wanted to linger over her body. This time he wanted all of her revealed to him.

"I want you inside me *now,* Diego. Please…" she said, her words a sensuous whisper.

Gritting his teeth, he clasped her wrists and stopped her. "No."

Kim blinked, felt a tightening in her throat.

It was the cruelest word in the English language. She sagged against him, her breath coming in choppy little puffs. It was a good thing his hard body was still supporting her or she would have sagged to the floor. She hid her face in his rising and falling chest, loath to reveal the tears burning at the backs of her eyelids.

He lifted her into his arms. Only when he lowered her onto the bed, on top of the covers, did she open her eyes again. He stood over her, his tight features set into a stony mask of spine-tingling…*resolve.* That was the only word for it.

What she saw in the tight set of his mouth, in the lingering heat in his hungry gaze, set all her internal alarms ringing.

His jaw set, he trailed his gaze over her slowly, from the top of her hair to her pink toenails, without missing an inch in the process. Something flitted into it and a flutter began in the pit of her stomach.

She was still clothed, even though the upper curves of her breasts were visible over her bra and her shorts were bunched up against her upper thighs.

He disappeared and then reappeared on the bed in the blink of an eye. With something in his hand. "Take off your clothes."

Her breaths came quick and rushed. The pink handcuffs

looked absolutely flimsy in his large hands. An unrelenting throb, a tremble, started in her. Pushing back with her heel, she tried to roll away from him. He didn't let her.

With her ankle in his free hand, he flicked his wrist and she slid down the bed, her legs now trapped between his knees.

A dark smile full of sinful promises curved his mouth. The handcuffs dangled in the air above her. "I want to see every inch of you, lick and kiss every inch of your skin. I want you incoherent with pleasure."

She shook her head, her mouth dry as a desert. His words had the most arousing effect on her. A slow, wicked pull began pulsing at her sex and she clutched her thighs together.

It wasn't enough that she had surrendered. She had to surrender *everything.* His words and her thoughts collided, her mind and her body clashed, even as an illicit thrill shot through her.

"No."

He shrugged, sitting back on his haunches. "My way or no way. Last offer, *gatinha.* Give up your control or I'm walking out the door."

There was a savage satisfaction, a grating pride in his words, that irked her.

She wanted to say, *Fine.* Slide off the bed and walk away. The word trembled on her lips. The sensible part of her was screaming at her to walk away. But what had all these years of being careful and logical brought her?

A crushing loneliness and nothing else.

She nodded, unable to give words to her acceptance.

His teeth were bared in a smile, gleaming with unabashed hunger.

Sliding back on the bed, trembling with a host of conflicting emotions, she unhooked her bra and shrugged it off.

A hungry groan was torn out of Diego and it shuddered around them.

He seemed to freeze right in front of her, drinking her in. Need knotted her nipples and moved incessantly lower. Gritting her jaw, she lay back against the bed and slowly peeled off her shorts in one movement.

He leaned forward and she drew in a sharp breath, her fingers halting on the edge of her panties. He clasped her wrists and tugged her arms upward. His shirt grazed her nipples, setting her skin ablaze. The hem of his jeans rubbed against her belly. She groaned and almost bucked off the bed, the delicious friction setting her skin on fire.

He neatly clamped her wrists with the handcuffs and moved back to his knees. "Turn around and lie facedown," he threw at her roughly, before sliding off the bed.

She bristled at his command, even though the hoarse note in his words, the way he moved away from her as though he didn't trust himself, sent a wave of feminine power rippling through her.

CHAPTER TEN

"CHOCOLATE OR STRAWBERRY?"

The question from across the room was fraught with unsatisfied hunger, mirroring her own. The soft Egyptian cotton chafed against her breasts and her skin. She let out a shaky breath.

"I have a choice?"

Silence—waiting, threatening—met her.

She shut her eyes, clutched the sheets with her fingers and mumbled "Chocolate…" Every second he didn't touch her was reducing her into a mindless state of anticipation and need.

She didn't know what she had expected—didn't know what his question even meant. It was definitely *not* the hot slide of his oil-slick palms over her back.

The massage oil.

She groaned as he rubbed at the knots in her shoulder. The scent of dark chocolate combined with his own, infiltrating every pore of her. His calluses abraded her skin, sparking tiny pinpricks of pleasure all over.

Done with the knots in her shoulders, his hands moved down, over her lower back, lower still to her buttocks. She closed her eyes and savored the sensation as they traveled over her buttocks, her thighs, her calves and even her feet.

They pulled and kneaded, rubbed and stroked, until every muscle in her was pliant and boneless. Her throat was raw with the sounds she made. She felt as if she was floating on clouds.

But he didn't stop.

And suddenly the tempo of his touch changed.

A different kind of pleasure slithered over her skin. Her mouth dried up. Her breath hitched in her throat.

Even his breathing seemed different, shallower, the strokes of his fingers more calculated.

A heat flush was overtaking every inch of her as he pushed her thighs the tiniest inch apart.

His slick hands molded over her thigh muscles. With new tension replacing old knots, she breathed hard. He tugged her panties down. She shuddered and struggled to move.

"Relax, *pequena*."

His command was gruff, curt.

She felt the slide of his hot mouth, open and scorching against the base of her spine. She moaned—a guttural sound that filled the cabin.

He scraped his teeth over one buttock. She clenched her thighs, trying to catch the ache there. With his huge palm between her thighs, he didn't give her that satisfaction.

She whimpered, ready to beg. "Please, Diego…just—"

"No, *gatinha*. Remember—my rules, my way."

His words elicited an erotic thrill from her that she had no way to control. Sliding his left hand beneath her tummy, he pulled her up a little, while his right hand steadily but slowly crept toward her sex.

An electric current sizzled along her nerves. She bit her lower lip hard, striving to catch the groan that was tearing out of her.

"Let go of your lip," he ordered, his voice guttural.

She shook her head in denial, or something like it.

He snuck a finger into her sex. Millions of nerve endings flared to life.

She flinched from the pleasure and then shivered all over, her toes curling into the bed.

Dear God, what was he doing to her?

She was draped over his hand like a rag doll, *everything* open and visible to him. She had never felt so vulnerable and so out of control. And yet she couldn't wait for him to do whatever he wanted with her.

His hand reached her curls, delved through her folds. She was aching for his touch, for the pressure that would send her over.

"*Droga,* but you're so wet and ready."

A scream built in her chest and she trembled from head to toe. "Please, Diego…" she whispered on a sob.

Another finger joined the first inside her sheath. She rubbed herself into his touch and heard his groan.

His fingers reached finally and stroked her clitoris. "Come for me, *gatinha.*"

She opened her mouth and breathed in jerkily. Pleasure built as he moved his fingers faster, inside and out, the heel of his palm rubbing against her with every movement. She closed her eyes, heat gathering momentum in her pelvic muscles, her groans sounding erotic.

Until he pressed down with his thumb and forefinger and set fire to that aching bundle of nerves.

She cried out as she orgasmed violently, white lights exploding behind her eyes, her breath hitching somewhere between the base of her throat and her lungs, her body fraying with the assault of pleasure, her mind utterly soaked with satisfaction.

The sound of her climax, rasping and throaty, wrenched a tormented answering shudder from Diego. He placed his palm on her lower back as the tremors in her body slowly subsided and then pulled her up to her knees gently. The scent of her arousal was thick in the air he breathed. Her skin was warm to the touch, with a faint sheen of sweat on it. Her locked hands lay in front of her. Her neck was thrown back against his shoulder.

His erection nestled into the curve of her buttocks. He rubbed himself against her and groaned, his shaft aching with need.

She felt so breakable in his rough hands, and the receding shudders in her slender body, her nudity, revealed a fragility that she hid under her perfection.

He pressed an open-mouthed kiss just above the indent of her buttocks and she tautened like an arrow. She tasted of chocolate and sweat. He trailed kisses upward, tasting and licking her, until he reached the graceful curve of her neck.

He opened his mouth and bit the tender flesh there. A moan rumbled out of her. She struggled against the handcuffs.

"Unlock them, Diego."

Her words were a raw, needy whisper. His stomach muscles tightened into hard rocks.

"I like you like this, *minha esposinha*," he said, uncaring that he sounded like the dirty thug he was. He pushed her hair away from her face and licked the seam of her ear.

Her response was a delicious tremble. "You're still fully dressed."

He moved his right forearm until his palm lay flat against her belly. She sucked in a sharp breath. He pushed her back onto the bed and joined her, lying on his side. She went without a sound. He laughed.

A delicate pink dusting her cheeks, she tried to cross her arms over her breasts and the triangle of curls that stole his breath.

She glared at him. "What?"

"I really like you all pliant and naked like this. All mine to do whatever I want with."

"Undo the cuffs, Diego," she said, with a hint of pleading in her words now.

He smiled and slid his palm up toward one breast, kneaded the soft flesh.

She closed her eyes on a long exhale and twisted to the side. As if she would deny him access. He stood up from the bed and eyed the dips and valleys of her body, need yanking relentlessly at his groin.

He shed his clothes quietly and rejoined her on the bed.

"Are your breasts already fuller, *gatinha?*" he asked, his words slurring around his tongue. "You're not quite showing, but I see the signs." He kissed the curve of her hip. "Here." He planted another one on her stomach. "Here."

Her gaze flew open, stroked over his naked body with a swift greed that set his teeth on edge. "You're still punishing me for walking away, aren't you?"

"I'm not. I adore seeing you naked, searching for the small little changes in your body that my children might already be causing."

She swallowed visibly, her gaze filled with a dark fear.

"I prefer to lie in bed with you and savor every inch of you instead of screwing you against the wall."

A single tear rolled out of her eye and he caught it with his mouth. It knocked the breath from his lungs. He palmed her face and forced her to look at him. "If you want me to stop—?"

She shook her head, the remaining unshed tears making her eyes twinkle like precious stones. "I'm...*glad* that it's your children inside me, Diego."

He felt a strange tightness in his chest as he captured her mouth again. Even the erotic pull of her mouth wasn't enough to dilute the disappointment that slashed through him. He'd had the feeling she had meant to say something else. But, as usual, she had kept it to herself.

And why the hell was he hanging on to each word of

hers like a faithful little dog? He needed to keep this on *his* terms.

He palmed her breast and felt a shudder go through him as the pebbled tip rasped against his palm. Her moan, almost bordering on a sob, filled his ears. His fingers looked worse than rough around the puckered nipple. He flicked it with the pad of his thumb and she pushed herself into his hand.

He kept his gaze on her, the sounds she made at the back of her throat, the lust that she couldn't hide from him, bleeding into the air around him, giving him unparalleled satisfaction.

She was his wife. She was going to be the mother of his children. This strong, brilliant, stubborn woman, who was worried that she didn't care about the babies in her womb, she needed him, needed something only he could give her.

In that moment she was unraveled at his touch, a hair trigger away from exploding with pleasure again.

Desire was a feral pounding in his veins. He hardened a little more, heat billowing from his very skin.

Nothing but her short gasp could have stopped him, so intent was he on losing his mind in her body and its softness.

"What is it, *pequena?*"

Her gaze took a few seconds to focus on him. She wiggled her handcuffed wrists and scrunched her nose. "They're beginning to hurt now."

He unlocked them instantly.

The next moment was a blur to his lust-soaked brain. As soon as he took the handcuffs off her she rolled away from him.

But he was in no mood for games or smiles. Somewhere between rubbing oil onto her body and seeing her naked he had begun losing control of himself again, started losing a small part of himself again. And he was damned if he'd let her take anything he wasn't willing to give.

"Come here, Kim," he said arrogantly.

Her gaze widened. She hadn't obviously missed the dark edge to his words. But of course she didn't heed his warning. She never did. It was always a battle of wills with her.

"Make me."

Kim squealed as Diego trapped her neatly on the bed. She threw punches. Not one fazed him. She even aimed her leg for a swift kick. It was too late.

He held her beneath him, his body a blazing furnace of tightly controlled desire.

He bent his mouth and took her nipple in his mouth. She lost the capacity for all coherent thought. He suckled at it—deep, long pulls that instantly sent pangs of need arrowing down to her sex—while his erection throbbed against her thighs.

She bucked off the bed, a throaty moan ripped from her throat. She snuck her hands into Diego's hair and held him there. He softly blew on the nipple and turned his attention to the other one. He rolled it between his fingers, rasped his stubble against the sensitive underside. She was ready to climax again.

She moved her legs restlessly and the rasp of his hair-roughened leg against hers sent sensations spiraling inside her. He closed his lips on the nipple and tugged it between his teeth. It was beyond bearable, bordering on pain-pleasure.

"I want to touch you, Diego," she pleaded, pushing him back, her hands on his shoulders. He didn't budge an inch.

He continued the assault with his mouth, trailing hot, wet kisses between her breasts, toward her stomach. Every inch of her skin that he kissed felt as if it was waking up from a long slumber.

The minute she felt his breath on her thighs she decided enough was enough. She rolled to slip from under him, a smile stretching her mouth from ear to ear.

Before he could stop her, she pushed him back on the bed and lay atop him from head to toe, her breath shaking in and out of her. Their mingled groans filled the silent cabin.

The rasp of her skin against his, the friction, was incomparable. Her breasts rubbed against his chest. His erection pressed into her belly. Her legs tangled with his.

Without giving him a moment to breathe, she pressed her mouth to his.

And she didn't do it tenderly. She gave the kiss everything she had in her, infusing her touch with every little emotion she had never been able to put into words and never could. She traced his lush lower lip with her tongue, nipped the moist inside, sucked his tongue into her mouth, rubbing herself against him like a cat.

God, whatever she did, she couldn't stop rubbing against him.

He breathed out on a hiss, his muscles shifting and pressing into her.

"You're going to be the death of me," he whispered as she dragged her mouth down to his neck.

He sounded utterly on edge, and she liked him like that. She bit his nipple and his fingers tightened on her arms.

She moved down and the friction of their sweat-slick bodies threatened to drive her crazy. She rubbed herself over his erection. He growled.

She dragged the tip of her tongue over the hard ridges of his stomach. He roared.

She clasped her fingers around his shaft and slid her fist up and down. Sweat shimmered on his brow. He jerked his hips into her touch, his stuttering breathing filling her ears. She bent and licked the swollen head, the taste and scent of him sending pulsing tingles straight to her wet core.

She laid her palm flat against his flinching abdominal muscles and licked the head again.

His upper body shot up off the bed, and before she could blink he'd tugged her boneless body until she was straddling him.

He grabbed her hips and entered her—slowly, hotly, precisely—until all she could feel was his possession. She clamped her arms around him so his face burrowed into her breasts as he pulled himself up.

A billion nerves jumped into life as their hips bumped into each other.

She dug the tips of her fingers demandingly into his rock-hard shoulders. She opened her eyes, ready to beg for more—and froze.

His gaze was studying her raptly, glittering with raw intensity, as though he saw into her very soul and found her disappointingly wanting. It was a sensation she couldn't shed, a feeling she couldn't shake.

But she was damned if she'd let it spoil the most precious moment of her life.

She kissed his mouth and moved swiftly off him.

And pushed herself back onto him.

They both groaned, the sounds needy, desperate, on edge.

She bent her head and bit his shoulder, digging her teeth into the muscle none too gently. It was all the signal he needed, apparently.

With a rough groan he reversed their positions, until he was on top of her. Throwing her legs over his shoulders, he thrust into her, harder, faster, until neither of them could see clearly, until neither could even breathe properly, until their bodies were ready to jump out of their shells.

She came with an unchecked scream that was torn out of her on a surge of need. Pleasure rocked through her—

waves and waves of unrelenting pressure that splintered and spread through every inch of her.

With one final thrust, Diego collapsed over her.

Eventually, even though it felt like forever, the pleasure waves receded, bringing in their wake painful realization. As though there was always a price for such life-altering joy as she had found in his arms.

She was in love with Diego. She always would be.

Had she ever been out of love with him really? It was a simple truth, as simple and soul-wrenching as the babies growing inside her.

Every inch of her wanted to retreat, hide, until she could come to terms with the terrifying truth. She needed to prepare herself, needed to set expectations for herself. She couldn't let it make her weak.

She couldn't let her love for him define her existence.

Diego felt Kim stiffen even before he pulled out of her. But he refused to let her hide from him. Not after the most intense orgasm of his life.

But when had it been anything less than explosive with her?

Still joined with her, he tumbled onto his back and pulled her with him until they were both lying sideways. He cupped her breast and kissed the upper curve of it, unable to resist the urge.

She opened her eyes with a helpless moan, dark chocolate pools swimming with desire. And yet there was a shadow of retreat, too.

"No, no, no," he whispered, putting his free hand on her temple and pressing.

She half smiled, every bit of it reluctant and torn from her. "No, what?"

He tapped her temple with his finger. "No thinking."

The shadows disappeared from her gaze and her mouth curved into a wide smile. He felt something loosen in his gut.

"No thinking, huh? That's like asking you…"

He raised his brow, urging her on.

"Like asking you to not be *sexy*." She raked her nails over his abdomen and he sighed with pleasure. "Although if you are naked like this I can't *actually* think."

He laughed. He really liked her like this. And not just because she was naked and sexy and it drove him crazy with desire. But because an inherent part of her—a side of her he rarely if ever saw—was exposed to him when they made love.

This intimacy, he realized slowly, was something she guarded closely—as she did all her feelings. It was something she had shared only with him. Primal satisfaction beat through him at the realization.

"Then we will be naked all the time. I mean, if that's what it takes to have a happy marriage I'm up for it."

She laughed, and the rich sound surrounded him.

He moved his hands toward her breasts and cupped them. "You were right. All this sophistication—it's just on the outside. Beneath it I'm an old-fashioned, chauvinistic man."

"Yeah?" she said, challenge glinting in her gaze. But her gaze dropped as he flicked a hard nipple with his fingers, her breathing becoming sharp.

"Yeah. I would like my wife to not think too much—even if she *is* one of the most brilliant women I have ever met. I would like to protect my wife from the big, bad world—even though she's the strongest woman I have ever met. I would like to be the only man—or the only *equipment*," he amended quickly, and she laughed, "that is allowed to touch her. I would like to be the only one who can—"

"Tie her up in knots? Make her forget right or wrong?

Turn her world upside down and generally plunge her life into chaos?"

His heart pounded so hard in his chest that he wondered if it would burst out of him.

"You already do all that and more to me, Diego."

Before he could pull in his next breath she pushed him onto his back and straddled him. With sure movements she wrapped his fingers around him and guided him inside her wetness as though she had blurted out too much…as though she didn't want him to linger over her words.

Once she started to move over him, her high breasts moving softly with her movements, her eyes drooping to half-mast with need, he forgot everything but the lust driving him to the edge.

He thrust upward in rhythm with her movements, he pulled himself up as her tempo increased. He pulled her nipple into his mouth and tugged at it with his teeth.

And she exploded around him, her muscles contracting and pulling at him. He thrust one more time into her and hit his own orgasm. He jerked his hips into her for every inch of pleasure she could give him, but something else was fueling the pleasure breaking out all over him.

CHAPTER ELEVEN

SITTING ON THE terrace overlooking the Brazilian coast, Kim ran her hands over her bare arms. The evening sky glittered with stars and the breeze carried a hint of the exotic flowers that were native to the island, which was an ecological paradise.

The past ten days she had spent here had flown by in a whirl, and they had been the best days of her life.

She saw Diego most days, except when he made trips to Rio di Janeiro. He made a lot of those—even though he was often back before she'd realized he was gone.

He didn't inform her about his schedule and she was still too new at this…whatever *this* was—to ask him to share. But the time they did spend together was becoming more and more precious to her.

Two days into their stay she had taken a trip around the island with Miguel, who had joined them a day after they arrived. She had met four young men, ranging from Miguel's eighteen-year-old best friend to a hulking brute of a boy whose age was indeterminate. And that was when she'd realized the truth.

Diego was doing everything he possibly could to get as many kids out of the street gang he himself had been a part of and bring them here. He was giving them honest work to do, showing them a different way of life. Some came willingly in search of a something better, and some, like

Miguel, who had seen too much violence already, didn't believe a better world existed.

She had thought Diego obsessed with wealth, determined to take everything he thought the world had denied him. She couldn't have been more wrong. She'd felt an insane urge to shout to the world what an honorable man he was, how wrong the media's perception of him was. So she had started a project with Miguel's help, excited to be doing something for Diego.

He might think himself damned, but with each passing second Kim could only see the good, the honor in Diego. And fall deeper into love with him.

Only being in love was just as horrible as she remembered it to be.

Not that she didn't enjoy the attention he showered on her. She had never been so pampered in her life. Forget pampered—no one had ever even so much as cooked a meal for her.

She walked on white beaches every day, swam in the infinity pool that edged from the villa into the ocean, napped for an hour every afternoon. The third day after their arrival Diego had even taken her on a hot air balloon ride over the island. It had been the most wonderful time she'd had.

He had shown her the exotic flora on the island, the place where construction had begun on a house for the teenagers he was bringing over. They had even seen Miguel and the other kids playing soccer on a vast expanse of untouched land.

Anything she asked for, she had it in a few hours—like the state-of-the-art camcorder she had requested.

He even had Miguel watch over her when he was busy, and the little punk seized her laptop every day after an hour, as though she was on the clock.

It had taken a couple of days but she had gotten over her panic about her company. Her staff were experts at what they did; of course they could manage without her for a couple of weeks.

She should feel on top of the world. And she did in those split seconds when she could stop obsessing and let the tight leash she kept on herself go.

Her day, from dawn to dusk, was spent wondering why he didn't kiss her again, what was stopping her from crawling into his bed—wherever it was that he slept. She was tired of waiting for him to make a move when all she wanted was to surround herself with him.

She wanted him, and she was pretty sure, from the way his hungry gaze ate her up, he wanted her. Tonight she would...

All her intentions disintegrated into dust when he walked onto the terrace. With his BFF in tow.

Jealousy burned like a blaze in her chest. She trembled from head to toe. The strength of it was feral. It pummeled her muscles into action and she got up in a sudden movement that made her lightheaded. She clutched at the wrought-iron railing.

Just the sight of him with Marissa was enough to burn a hole through her heart.

For the first time in over a week Kim had no appetite for dinner. Even though Anna had prepared everything the way Kim liked.

She smiled and nodded, answered with yes or no for the first half hour, pushing her food halfheartedly around on her plate. The other woman—or *was* she the other woman in this case?—was nothing but polite, inquiring after Kim's health, how she was enjoying her stay on the island.

There was only so much Marissa could do to squelch the awkwardness while Kim stayed resolutely mute. But what could she say?

She felt such an influx of emotions—jealousy roped

with guilt that she had destroyed this woman's life with one single action, a hot rush of anger toward Diego for subjecting them all to this—she was literally stupefied into speechlessness.

Eventually Marissa switched to Portuguese, and Kim was almost grateful for the snub. She waited another ten minutes before she excused herself and fled back to the terrace.

Loneliness churned through her and she suddenly missed Liv with an ache. She needed her irrepressible twin so much right now. Because her life was in tatters if *this* was how being in love was going to feel.

A soaring high one minute and a gut-wrenching low the next.

It was early evening the next day when Diego found Kim walking along the beach, a couple of miles from the villa. He made a quick call.

This part of the island was even more untouched than the other side. Pristine white sands, turquoise waters—he loved this view. This island was the one thing he owned that gave him the utmost satisfaction and joy at what he had achieved in life.

It was a place with nothing but sky and acres of land around him. The one thing he had craved for so long. Somewhere that wasn't a ditch to call his own. Now Miguel, and others like him, could enjoy the freedom that came from knowing their very lives *didn't* depend on their ability to throw punches and fight dirty.

Not that he had ever stopped. Now it was just for different things.

Today the view didn't hold his interest. And he had a feeling the quiet contentment he had felt over the past week or so had been more to do with the solitary figure half a mile in front of him than his success in purchasing the island that he had wanted for so long.

To break that spell he had brought Marissa. He could have caught up with her on his next trip to Rio. But he knew she'd wanted to see the island. And he was loath to change anything in his life just because Kim was in it now.

That was the only way to keep this in check. Only Kim had looked as if he had slapped her last night.

It had taken everything he'd had in him to not chase after her when she had left for the terrace halfway through dinner. Instead he had spent the evening with Marissa, going over the last few legalities. Even her update that visa issues were now taken care of for two more boys like Miguel hadn't been enough to keep his mind from Kim.

And yet he had fought the pull.

He didn't even have a clear idea why. As each day passed with her he had felt an increasing sense of uncertainty creeping into his thoughts. As to how much he enjoyed her company, how much he looked forward to seeing her in the morning, how much he enjoyed it when she pored over a financial report with him and came up with a solution in two minutes flat.

He had learned early on that anything that felt that good always came with a high price.

He tucked his hands into the pockets of his trousers and came to a standstill, watching her. Not his heart, though. It pounded extra hard in his chest.

The utter silence, punctured only by the ocean's waves, cocooned them, weaving its own magic.

She stood barefoot in the sand, the ocean lapping at her feet.

Her slender back, skin glowing in the sun, was pure temptation marred only by two yellow strings tied at the neck and then down lower. His gaze followed the curve of her back to the dip. A sarong-style wrap hugged her pert behind. Her long legs were only visible again from her knees.

He released a shaky breath. He had purposely pulled himself back these past few days, held back through sheer will. He didn't want to fall headlong into his desire for her again, to forget the right and wrong of the situation—forget himself.

He wanted the comfortable camaraderie they had slipped into to last. He wanted something stable for his children, and for the first time since she had told him that she was pregnant, for the first time on this island, he felt the goodness of what they had in his bones.

This felt right. This felt good. And he would do anything to keep it like that.

The line of her shoulders tightened infinitesimally. Her hands wrapped around herself and she stiffened, holding herself aloof from the world.

It was enough to burst the bubble of tranquility he had felt just a second ago. Tension curled his muscles and his mind geared up for whatever fight she was going to throw his way, his body exulting in the thrill shooting through his blood.

She turned and met his gaze.

He felt the intensity of her look as if she had run those long fingers over him. His muscles were flexing and rearing for her touch. Lust rocketed through him, tightening every muscle with fiery need.

Her lustrous hair slapped across her face. Her bikini top cupped her breasts just as he wanted to. He couldn't deny they were looking rounder. She had put on some weight, was losing that gaunt, over-worked look. And she had that first blush of pregnancy he had overheard Anna mentioning to her.

It was in the slight flare of her hips, in the fullness of her breasts, in the healthy flush of her skin. Her stomach, though not yet round, was beginning to grow. He trailed his gaze over her, enjoying the sheer eroticism of looking at her.

She was the sexiest woman he had ever seen, and her innate modesty made her even more appealing. Even now she was oblivious to her effect on him, on his self-control, as her overactive mind whizzed through something.

"Do you miss being with her?"

Diego blinked. For a second he didn't understand her question. "*Droga,* I knew I shouldn't have left you alone for so long. You're ripe for a fight, aren't you?"

"That's ridiculous."

"You are much more comfortable when we're fighting, when you can peg me into whatever box you can. We have been laughing, generally enjoying each other's company, for over a week now. So of *course* it's time to draw the lines again."

"I...I'm serious, Diego."

He didn't miss whatever it was he had once shared with Marissa. It had been a comfortable relationship they had both fallen into whenever something had gone wrong in their lives—the one good thing that had stood firm despite every hardship they had faced.

He just wished he had realized sooner that it had meant so much more to Marissa than it had to him. What he felt for Kim—a crazy obsession that knew no right or wrong— he had never had with any other woman in life.

Nothing like the fizzle of anticipation roaring in his blood as she came closer, nor the tightening in his gut every time he thought he had finally reached the core of her and then she retreated behind her shell again.

She came to a halt right in front of him. Her scent teased his nostrils. Hot arousal was inching across his skin.

"You don't have to spare my feelings. I can take it," she said.

Curiosity blazed like a forest fire through him. "Does that mean it would hurt you if I said I do miss her?"

"Yes," she replied, her mouth a tight line.

Was it downright sadistic of him to *enjoy* the fact that she could be hurt by his actions? That he had a hold over her, however tenuous?

"I couldn't trust myself to not lose it right in front of her. That's why I left. I will understand if you...want me to leave."

He cursed—a filthy word his mother would have washed out his mouth for. "What the hell does that mean?" At her grating silence, he answered. "I don't miss her."

"Then why is she here? Who are you trying to punish by pushing us all together? Yourself or me?"

He frowned. "You want me to cut her out of my life? Tell her she has no part in it now that you are here? She's the one person who has stood by me my whole life. Whether I was a success or a failure, whether I was being a sanctimonious bastard or not. What do you expect me to do? Tell her—?"

Kim shook her head, feeling sick to her stomach. She got it now. Marissa was the *constant* whereas Kim was the *variable*—the one who could disappear from his life any minute.

Maybe even the one he could leave behind when he didn't want her anymore?

"I don't know," she said, her anxiety spilling into her words. "All I want to know is whether you'll give this... us...a real chance or not."

"And bringing a friend of mine here means I won't?" He smiled. "Is this you being jealous, *gatinha?*"

Kim flinched. "I'm sorry. I don't know what came over me. I have no right to—"

He tugged her around. "Yes, you do. You have every right to ask me whatever you want to. You might not always like the answer. It could be worse than what you lose by keeping silent. Why do you *do* that?"

"What?"

"Walk away silently."

She tried to shy her gaze away from him. "I don't know what you're talking about."

"Yes, you do. Even last time on the island, when I said I was done with you, you didn't utter a word. You should have called me a bastard right then. Instead you left without a word. You fight more for your company than you do for yourself."

"If I don't ask anything of you, don't expect anything of you, you can't hurt me."

He shook his head. "It is never that simple."

"It's the only way to survive."

"Who hurt you?"

She tried to turn away from him but he wouldn't let her. This was not a conversation she wanted to have. "No one hurt me, Diego. However, you will be disgusted by the depths of selfishness I can fall to."

His hands locking her in place, he looked into her eyes. "Nothing you do or have done will ever make me despise you. Make me angry, yes. Drive me crazy, yes… But disgust me…? *No.* Haven't I showed you that already?"

"The night before my mother left I found her note."

"A note?"

Every inch of her shook just remembering that night. "It was one line. Addressed to my father. She was leaving him and taking Liv with her."

Leaving her behind.

She had gone to her mother's room to check on her, to inform her of what her father had planned for the next day, to tell her that she had taken care of everything needed for a small party at their house.

Instead she had found a small bag sitting on the floor

of the closet. It had contained her mother's jewelry, cash, her passport and—the thing that had sent a shiver down Kim's spine—Liv's passport. For a frantic minute she had emptied the bag, looking for her own passport, her lungs constricting painfully.

It hadn't been in that bag.

Wondering if her mother had made a mistake, her head reeling from what it meant, she had walked to the bed and found the note scribbled on her mother's stationery.

It had been the worst moment in her life—sitting there, wondering what she had done wrong, how she could have acted any different, why her mother would choose to take Liv but not her…

Her vision blurred. The same confusion, the same utter desolation sprang inside her at the memory. The words she hadn't dared to speak aloud, the thoughts that wouldn't leave her alone even after all these years, the fears she hadn't shared with another soul, poured out of her on a wave of uncontrollable pain.

"For as long as I can remember I did everything I could to shield her from my father. I always stayed strong for her. I stayed by her bed when she was ill. I never once asked her for anything, Diego. And in the end she—" her voice broke, her insides twisting into a mass of pain.

Diego's rough palms on her cheeks, the familiarly comforting scent of him, pulled her out of the depths of despair. He forced her to look at him.

"Tell me you confronted her, Kim. Tell me you demanded to know why."

"No. And I didn't beg her to take me, too, if that's what you want to hear." Her throat felt as if pieces of glass were stuck in it. "I threatened to go to my father with the note if she went anywhere near Liv. I stayed awake by Liv's side all night. And my mother…she…left sometime during the night. But you're right. I *am* an unfeeling, selfish bitch."

"You did nothing wrong." His words were a frustrated growl.

"No? You see, I was determined to not let her rob the one person who loved me from my life. Except you know what…?"

His stomach churning with a vicious force, Diego watched Kim. She walked away from him, trembling from head to toe, her words vibrating with pain.

"Liv paid for it. With our mother gone, my father turned his corrosive, controlling attention to *her*."

"You can't blame yourself for that. You were a child."

"He made her life miserable every single minute of every single day, Diego," she said, her fists locked by her sides. "There—are you disgusted now?"

How could he hate her for surviving when he would have done the same? She'd lived her life with the cards she had been dealt and made no excuses for it.

She slipped from him before he could tell her how much he understood, how that kind of hurt never died down.

She could have hated Olivia after her mother left. But she had been strong for both of them, had tried to shield her from their father when she had been nothing more than a teenager herself. And she thought there was nothing in her that felt…

He tugged her closer and wrapped his hands around her. She didn't relax immediately. He tightened his hold.

She smelled of the ocean and lemons and something undeniably *her*.

He stood holding her like that, running his fingers over her back. So many things rushed through him. Utter amazement at her strength robbed him of his ability to speak.

Walking away from her mother, from her father, from him—it was the only way she had survived.

A lump in his throat cut off his breath and he relaxed his hold on her.

Handling her was no different from handling a hurt teenager like Miguel, really. Miguel lashed out at the world in order to live through his pain, whereas Kim internalized everything to survive—pushed her own feelings and desires so deep inside she had pretty much cauterized herself against any hurt.

If his childhood had been hell, hers had been no better. Just a different kind of hell.

"You remind me of Miguel," he whispered, breathing her scent deep into his lungs.

She looked up at him, reluctance filling her gaze. "I don't know what to make of that."

"Whenever I see him in pain I want to hunt down everyone that's hurt him. It's the same way I feel right now. Instead of protecting you, your mother used you and Olivia as shields against her husband. She was not fit to be a mother. And I will throttle you if you compare yourself to her again."

Tears glazed her eyes.

He moved his palm to her stomach and felt his heart kick inside his chest. "Except I've never wanted to kiss Miguel, as I want to do you, every waking minute."

Kim blinked back the tears that prickled behind her eyes. His tenderness was unraveling her and she was terrified she would never be whole again, never be strong again.

Day by day, word by word, he had slowly peeled away all her armor. Her emotions were spilling and overflowing. It was both terrifying and exciting.

She shivered and scrunched closer to him. His arms were steel bands around her, his body a furnace of need and want. And for the first time in her life she felt wanted. As if her wishes mattered, as if *she* mattered. And not for her brains, for her accomplishments, but for the person she was beneath all that—scared and hurt and frozen.

She moved in his embrace and pressed her mouth to his chest. He rumbled beneath her touch.

"Come with me," he whispered.

Her smaller hand encompassed by his, she let him tug her whichever way he wanted.

They walked for about five minutes, the sand crunching under their feet.

She came to a sudden halt, dragging Diego to a stop along with her. Dusk was beginning to streak the sky orange above them and a custom-made cabana, its dark oak gleaming in the fading sunlight, stood about two feet from them, big enough to accommodate two people.

And narrow enough to squish them together.

Pristine white cotton sheets covered the opening, contrasting richly against the dark oak. Heat uncurled low in her belly, her legs threatening to collapse under her.

And that wasn't all.

A small table was set up in front of the cabana, with candles and dinner for two. A pink cardboard box with a small bow also sat on it. The curly "A" on top of it looked very familiar...

His hard body shifting behind her, Diego wrapped his arms around her, his strong legs supporting her own.

"That's a box from Angelina's in Paris." It was her favorite patisserie on the Champs d'Elysées.

Suddenly she knew what was in it. She turned to him, laughter bubbling out of her.

"Anna told me you've mentioned their pastries once or twice."

She met his laughing gaze. "How about a million times?"

"Happy Anniversary, *minha esposinha*."

Her breath hitched in her throat. It was the first thing that had hit her when she'd woken up this morning—the reason why she had wandered away so far from the villa.

It was the one date she had always taken off and spent at her apartment, reliving that day.

She nodded, struggling to speak past the lump cutting off her breath. Stretching on her toes, she pressed into him until his erection rubbed against her bottom.

He groaned and hugged her tighter.

"I don't want the pastry."

He licked the seam of her ear. Her skin was too fraught with need to contain her.

"What *do* you want, *querida?* Whatever it is, I will bring it to you."

"You," she said clearly, loud enough for anyone in the vicinity to hear. It wasn't all she actually wanted to say, though. "I want *you,* Diego."

Without waiting for his answer she dragged him toward the cabana, intent on showing him with her actions everything she still wasn't brave enough to put into words.

They tore off each other's clothes with frenzied movements, as though they were both aware of how fragile, how precious this moment of perfection was.

Pushing her back into the soft mattress, Diego stretched out on top of her, his taut muscles a heavenly weight over her. His mouth, his tongue, his caresses, *he* was everywhere—kissing her, licking her, tasting her, generally reducing her body to a writhing mass of sensations and needs. He didn't give her a minute to breathe.

She cried out loud, the raw sound clawing its way out of her throat, when he pulled her nipple deep into his mouth and suckled at it. His rough fingers tweaked its twin, and twangs of hot pleasure shot down between her legs.

He smelled of the ocean, his muscles taut and shifting under her touch. She sobbed incoherently when he rubbed her aching core with the heel of his palm while his mouth trailed wet kisses around her navel. Pleasure coiled low in her belly, tugging every nerve-ending inside her along for the ride. Her whole body was unfolding mindlessly in tune with his erotic strokes.

His hair-roughened legs rubbing against hers, he reversed their positions with one smooth movement until she was straddling him.

Her sex quivered with need as his erection rubbed against her folds, and a shiver inched its way all over her skin.

Putting her weight on her thighs, she resisted.

His face was all severe planes and rough angles in the fading light. His choppy breath bounced off of her skin, giving her goosebumps.

His mouth was tight, his gaze drugged with desire. "This is not the time for one of your arguments, *gatinha*."

She smiled at the way his words rolled over each other, his accent creeping into his words. She placed her palms on his thighs and the rock-hard muscles clenched under her touch.

He groaned—a guttural, painful sound—as she drew her palms upward a little, until the pads of her fingers were idly tracing the length of his erection.

Her mouth dry, she forced herself to put her thoughts into words. "I want you on top of me." Pushing her hands into her hair, she stretched innocently.

His gaze moved to her breasts. Naked hunger was etched into his face. "Why?"

She slid off him and stretched alongside him. He immediately turned toward her. "I'm going to start showing in a little while." He moved his palm to her stomach. "And I...we...in the coming months it's going to be awkward."

He frowned. "So you won't want to have sex anymore? Because being near you and not having it will kill me."

She laughed. God, she would never have enough of his piercing honesty. "I will. But today I want your weight over me as you enter me. I want to feel every inch of you plastered to me."

He didn't say anything. He just pulled her wrists up with one hand and kissed her mouth, plundering her. Kneeled between her legs. Pulled one leg over his shoulder. Covered every inch of her with him as he thrust into her.

She was already wet and ready for him. But something more than pure lust sang in her veins. Her breasts shifted against his chest as he moved inside her. Her stomach groaned under the weight of his muscles. Sweat beaded over his forehead and she licked his shoulder when he thrust again.

It was hard and crushing. Her breathing was ragged, her skin ablaze with need. The delicious friction of his thrusts awakened a billion nerve-endings in her groin muscles.

Sharp bursts of pleasure crested over her. Desire pooled low and intense in her pelvis. She sensed his control slipping, his desire taking over, just as hers did, and each thrust was more desperate and less measured. Each sound he made was rougher and filled with a delicious lack of control.

When they hit their climaxes and pleasure broke out all over her she knew nothing was going to protect her heart now. How stupid she had been to think she still had control over this—that she could withstand it without losing herself.

Her heart was Diego's now—*whatever* he wanted to do with it. And she couldn't help but hope, after everything they had been through together, that he wouldn't trample it.

CHAPTER TWELVE

IT HAPPENED WHEN they had almost reached the villa. The fact that it had been near midnight by the time they had finished with each other, *and* with dinner at the secluded spot, meant that the loud, strident peal from his cell phone shattered the peace, the moment of perfection.

Diego froze next to her, bringing them both to a grinding halt even before he picked it up. He literally froze—his body next to her and his hand around hers going from delicious warmth to dreadful cold in a second. The jarring tune blared again, and Kim realized why she had felt a shiver go down her spine that first time.

That ringtone was different from his usual one. Which meant he had set it up for a particular call. And he seemed to expect the worst.

He shifted to the side, almost as though hiding himself from her, and picked up his phone.

The conversation lasted two minutes—tops.

A curse flew from his mouth and Kim flinched. With a growl that had the little hairs on her neck standing, he hurled his cell phone. It fell into the ocean and sank in seconds with a little gurgle.

Leaving the most deafening silence around them.

His emotions floated over him like a dark cloud that cut off the intense physical connection she had felt with him only a few minutes ago. Like a signal of extreme danger to anyone who dared approach him.

Foreboding inched over her, her skin chilly in the balmy night air.

He stared into the ocean, his shoulders rattling.

She reached him quietly where he stood, with tension and aggression pouring out of every sinew of him. "Diego, what's going on?"

"He's dead."

The words landed around them with the intensity of an earthquake that shook everything. She swayed for a second, her gut trembling. She dug her toes into the sand, blindly seeking to root herself. "Who?" she asked, wishing her instincts could be wrong.

"Eduardo."

The anguish in him wound itself around her. "I'm so sorry, Diego."

"Multiple organ failure killed him."

"I—"

"But they are wrong."

Her tongue wouldn't move to form the words she wanted to ask. She was so terrified of everything crumbling. "What do you mean?"

"*I'm* the one who killed him. As surely as if I put my hands on his throat and choked the life out of him."

Kim gasped. The self-loathing in his words was unbearable to hear. The need to comfort him pounded in her blood. "What are you talking about? Eduardo loved you."

"And I used his love, his trust in me, to my advantage. He was already crumbling under the weight of my father's expectations. And you know what I did? I befriended him under false pretenses, gained access to the company's information and pulled it out from under him. My father had no choice but to hand it over to me. I told myself Eduardo was barely keeping it together anyway. And then, when you left, I wanted blood. I went from driven to obsessed. Instead of helping him, I pushed him into his own destruction. I should have known Eduardo was already using— should have known how close he was to breaking. By the time I did it was already too late. Are you *still* glad that it's my children you're carrying, *gatinha?*"

The words dug their claws into her.

"I am. Because you're not that man anymore, Diego. You never were. I see how you are with Miguel, what you've gone through to pull him from that life. Whatever culpability you have in Eduardo's death—if you have any—you have paid for it a million times over."

She moved toward him and folded her arms around his middle from behind. A tremor shook him and it crashed into her, his raw anguish churning her stomach.

Innocence. They had both never had it. And even without realizing it they had been drawn to each other. For the first time she felt the loss of it as keenly as he did.

She pressed her mouth to his shoulders, felt him shudder under her touch, felt him pull in a breath with the utmost effort.

She wanted to do everything she could to ease his pain. The intensity of how much she wanted to rocked through her. For a second she thought he might let her share his pain—for once let *her* support *him*.

"You have to forgive yourself. If you don't you'll—"

He walked away from her without a word.

His silence whipped at her hope. The weight of his guilt was a crushing weight on her own shoulders, even if he said it wasn't her fault.

Kim stood there watching him go, her hold on him just as slippery as the sandbanks holding the ocean at bay.

Kim didn't see Diego over the next couple of days. It was Miguel who informed her that he had gone to Sao Paulo to bury Eduardo, and that Marissa was by his side. It was Miguel who didn't leave her side for a minute, as though he could understand her mounting confusion.

Marissa was the one person Diego hadn't shut out of his grief. His friend had stayed by his side while Kim had watched from afar.

It hurt like nothing else in her life had—like a nail stuck under her skin, gouging into her flesh. And there was nothing she could do to change it

Would it be like this forever? She hated that feeling from the depths of her soul—hated that her happiness, her very state of mind, was dependent on whether Diego would ever smile at her again.

It was the same vicious circle of hell she had gone through when she had found her mother's note. What could she have done differently? What could she change within herself? It was a powerless, clawing feeling she couldn't shed.

She blinked back tears, disgusted by the feeble feelings. She missed him every minute of every day with an intensity that stole the breath from her lungs.

How could she live like this forever? Wanting to be more, needing to be more to him, but knowing that she could never change it?

She knew they had formed a bond in the past days. She knew, for all that her life had been an emotional desert, that what they shared had been special. But he would never love her. She would never amount to anything other than the mother of his children.

It was a truth she had already known, except now it felt excruciatingly unbearable.

Pain constricted her chest. Her lungs were collapsing under its crushing weight. She sank to her knees on the hardwood floor in her bedroom and hugged herself.

She couldn't live with him like this—forever wondering, waiting for the moment he decided she wasn't worth it, the moment he decided he was done with her.

Because he would. Sooner or later he would decide he only wanted his children. She would go mad waiting for that moment.

She had wanted this chance with him, but she didn't want it at the cost of losing her sanity, her will.

Diego couldn't believe the evidence of his own eyes. His gut kept falling lower and lower as he methodically checked each room through the villa. He left her room for last—like a coward postponing the moment of truth.

She has gone.

Miguel had texted him almost two hours ago. Because Miguel, unlike his pilot and the rest of the staff, had known something was wrong, had known her swift departure was something Diego wouldn't have agreed to if his life had depended on it.

Lost in his own world on the other side of the island, pushing himself through another rigorous workout, Diego had seen it too late.

His heart, if it was possible, felt as if it had come to a screeching halt. Because he had instantly known it wasn't a work emergency, as she had claimed to everyone else, or a tantrum because he had been avoiding her since he had heard Eduardo's news.

Kim didn't throw tantrums. She didn't argue, and she didn't fight back—she left quietly, as though he wasn't even worth a goodbye.

His helicopter was gone, his pilot was gone and Kim was gone. And yet he couldn't crush the fleck of hope holding him together.

It was the most pathetic feeling that had ever run through him. Right up there with the hope that had fluttered every time his mother had trotted him down to his father's house to beg for his help.

He arrived at the suite she had been using. The sheer curtains at the French windows flew in the silence. Crickets chirped outside on the veranda.

She hadn't left the room as spotless as she usually did. A couple of paperbacks were still on the bed.

The scent she used, lily of the valley, fluttered over the breeze toward him. Knocked him in the gut like a kick to his insides. He breathed deeply, trying to get the knot in his belly to relent.

A strange sense of déjà-vu descended on him. He looked at the bathroom, his heart in his throat, waiting for her to emerge from it as she had in the hotel suite that day. She would come out and turn her nose up at him. Challenge him. Rile him. And kiss him.

Breathing through the pain, he reminded himself that it would crest soon. It had to.

It didn't.

He rammed his fist into the nearby wall and roared a pithy curse.

Despite his best efforts, he was right where she had left him six years ago—he still wasn't enough for her. Why else would she leave without a word?

In the wake of that crushing realization came waves of roaring fury and unrelenting pain. He was damned if he'd let her go.

He would move heaven and earth to drag her back into his life. He would spend every last dollar he had and more on suing her for custody, using any legal means he had to tie her to him. He would destroy everything he had built — destroy himself if that was the price to make her his again.

He wanted her back in his life. And he would fall as low as needed.

* * *

He had just hung up with his lawyer when Miguel entered his office. He cast a long look at Diego, threw a file on his table, switched on the flatscreen TV and left.

Diego was about to turn off the TV when a familiar sight stopped him in his tracks. The pristine white beaches, the turquoise waters as a background, with Miguel in the fore-front, were *here*—on the island.

Stunned, he settled into the couch.

The documentary started with Miguel being asked questions about his past life. Diego could see the resentment in his face, past hurt playing shadows in his dark gaze, the effort it cost him to answer those questions.

He shivered as he realized it was Kim answering the questions. She walked Miguel through every tough question, her tone gentle as he revealed his horrible past

The questions then focused on his current life. His chest tightened and a warm energy flew in Diego's veins as she probed Miguel on how Diego had taken Miguel out of the street gang in Rio di Janeiro, how Diego had worked long days to get through to Miguel that violence wasn't the an-swer, how Diego had brought him to this island…

Tears burned in Diego's eyes as the short feature went on. As Kim interviewed the other two kids who had joined them last week.

And then it was her smiling face that filled his huge screen.

"The world should know of Diego Pereira's efforts to get these kids out of violent street gangs and toward a bet-ter life."

Her statement reverberated within him, shaking the rigid fear at the core of him loose.

He switched the television off, his heart pounding. She thought the world should know what he was doing. But he had never wanted the world's applause, the world's validation.

He had wanted it from *her,* had craved it. He had wanted to be worthy of the strong, brilliant, beautiful woman she was.

Feeling as though he was coming apart, he opened the file that Miguel had tossed at him.

The contents of the file blew him away. There were detailed plans for the infrastructure required to run a shelter for kids recovering from drug problems. There was a list of healthcare workers who had expertise in working with kids like Eduardo. A list of legalities and forms that needed to be fulfilled in order to begin such a program right there on the island.

It was detailed, precise and exactly what he had had in mind when he had bought the island. He had never revealed his plans to her. She couldn't have created a file that made her loss more apparent.

Every inch of him ached at the emptiness he felt. Had she been horrified by what he had driven Eduardo to?

Seeing Eduardo's body, seeing his own father, whom he had hated for so many years, his hatred blazing just as ever, had broken the hold he had kept on himself—had shown him what he couldn't achieve through wealth or power, however hard he fought.

All his life he had fought for everything he had. But he hadn't been able to make his mother happy before she died, he had never received his father's acknowledgment or praise and he hadn't been able to save Eduardo.

If he did anything to manipulate Kim now, if he fell any lower—even if it was because he loved her—he would probably only destroy her, as he had done Eduardo, and she had already suffered enough.

He closed his eyes and threw his head back. Grief

scratched at his throat, and his muscles were burning with
the need to fight, to bring her back into his life.

But he couldn't.

He couldn't force her to love him—not as he loved her.
With every breath in him. With every cell in him. And letting her go meant letting go of the dream he had looked for
with her and his children.

He had no doubt she would love their babies, whatever
her fears.

In the end, after everything he had done to get to this
stage in life, he was terrifyingly powerless again—and
alone with it all.

CHAPTER THIRTEEN

"ARE YOU GOING to avoid me for the rest of our lives?"

Kim drew a sharp breath, her fork freezing midway to her mouth, as Liv's words flew across the lounge like loaded missiles. She had been back in New York for a week now and had been dreading confrontation. But this wasn't one she had prepared herself for.

She had forgotten that Liv still had a key to her apartment. And she had been so lost in her own thoughts that she hadn't even heard the front door being opened.

Liv joined her at the dining table, her gaze brimming with concern—and something else. *Almost fear.*

"Hey, Liv."

She lifted her fork to her mouth and took a bite of pasta. She chewed on it, forcing herself to keep at bay the nausea that had been threatening all day. It had become worse the moment she had returned—as though her body had gone into fully fledged revolt the minute she had got off the plane from the island.

Away from Diego.

Liv pulled a chair out, sat down at the table and studied her.

"You look like hell, Kim. You shouldn't look like this."

Kim nodded, and ran her palm over her midriff. She raised her head and met Liv's gaze. "I just haven't been sleeping well. I have been taking good care of myself, Liv," she said guiltily. "I've cut down my hours. I've been eating lots." She pushed her chair back and hugged Liv. Hard. "*You* look wonderful, though."

Liv's arms tightened around her. "Please tell me this is just you being hormonal. Because you're scaring me."

Kim bit her lip, striving to hold back the raw ache in her throat. "You and Alex okay?" she said softly. Every time she saw one of them she felt the knot of guilt in her stomach relent a little. As different as they were, Alex was the perfect man for her sister.

If Diego hadn't stopped her Alex wouldn't have fallen in love with Liv, and *she* wouldn't have the babies growing in her womb… A shiver went over her.

"I'm not here to talk about Alexander and me."

Kim laughed and pulled back from her. "That means you're fighting again?"

Liv shrugged. "He's angry that I forged his signature on Emily's parental release form so that she can screentest for a movie role," she replied, a guilty blush stealing into her cheeks.

"*You forged his…?* God, Liv. I know how he is about his sister. How *could* you?"

"Acting's in her blood, Kim. She was going to do it whether he agreed or not. And Alexander…*when he loves someone*…it's just so…" She hesitated, a little shiver spewing into her words. "Emily doesn't realize how easily she can hurt him. And I would rather he be pissed off with me than—"

"Than be hurt by her?" Kim finished for Liv, her gut folding in on itself.

She stared at her twin, a fog falling away from her eyes. They looked similar, yet they were so different on the inside. Even before their mother had left Liv had always somehow understood their mother's pain.

Hadn't that always been the difference between them?

Liv's ability to put everything she loved before herself? To take that leap again and again, even if it pained her? To risk everything for love?

Kim had always assumed that *she* was the stronger one—the one in control, the one with no weaknesses. What if her strength had only been a self-delusion? Was she a coward after all? A coward who didn't believe herself worthy of being loved?

She had been so sure she loved Diego, but apparently only if there were no risks involved, only if she was sure that he would return her feelings.

"I'm worried about you, Kim," Liv said. "Alexander told me you asked him to recommend a good custody lawyer. And yesterday Diego came to see me."

"He did what?" Kim's fork clattered to the table. "He was in New York?" And he hadn't even called her.

Liv nodded, worry creasing her brow. "He…he wanted me to give you something. He said he didn't want you to open it alone. I think he's worried about you. When I asked him why he didn't do it himself, he said he was done running after you."

Liv opened her handbag and pulled out an envelope from it.

Fear curled up in her stomach and Kim braced herself.

He hadn't called her. He hadn't responded to her email. Every second of every day for the past week she had been on tenterhooks, waiting to hear something, *anything* from him. And she had a terrifying feeling about the contents of that envelope.

He was going to sue her for custody. He was going to take the babies away from her.

Just the passing thought was enough to plunge her into an abyss of panic. Her hands moved to her stomach and she shuddered. Her lungs felt as if they were seizing up on her.

She sagged to the floor and tucked her head between her legs.

Her palm on Kim's back, Liv whispered something, but Kim could hear nothing past the terror clawing through her. She couldn't even bear the thought of being forced to part with her children, the thought of not seeing them every day for the rest of her life.

How cold-hearted had her mother been to walk away so easily from them? Kim couldn't imagine making that choice if her life depended on it.

Maybe she would have a little girl with a golden gaze and a distinct nose like Diego's, and a boy with jet-black hair and a penchant for fighting. She would love her kids no matter what life threw at her. She would spend every minute…

A choked sound fell from her mouth.

There it was. The connection. The joy she had wanted to feel for so long. She closed her eyes and gripped the feeling closer to her heart. She curled up on the floor and gave in to the tears scratching her throat.

She couldn't share it with Diego. Couldn't tell him of the joy overflowing within her at the thought of the children they had created together. Couldn't tell him she finally understood what he had experienced from the minute she had told him about the pregnancy.

And now he was going to take them away from her.

Liv joined her on the floor and hugged her. "God, Kim. What are you doing to yourself?"

Kim wiped her tears and steadied herself. At least now she had the strength to fight for her kids—she couldn't expect Diego to give up his rights, but she was damned if she would either.

"If you don't want to open this now—"

She shook her head. "No. Better to get this over with…"

Casting her a worried look, Liv tore the envelope. Her mouth tight, she scanned the documents rapidly.

"This is a motion to start divorce proceedings. You're to have full custody and there's a note requesting minimum visitation rights to the...*children?*"

Kim gasped, every inch of her trembling with relief and shock.

"Wait... What does he mean *children?* Oh my God, you're having twins?"

Clutching Liv's hand, Kim nodded. Her vision was blurred. Her head felt dizzy. Delayed shock was setting in.

He was divorcing her. He was giving her full custody...

Liv skimmed through the papers in her hand again. "He will never contest your custody rights in any way. He..."

Saliva pooled in Kim's mouth, followed by a wave of nausea pushing its way up her throat. She kept her hand on her stomach.

Liv threw the papers on the table and knelt in front of her. She squeezed Kim's fingers, her gaze filled with shock. "It's so strange, isn't it? After everything he did to get you into his life, he's agreeing to all this."

An empty chill pervaded Kim's limbs, sucking out every ounce of emotion from her. *This was it.* "He's finally given up on me."

"What?"

"He's finally realized I'm not worthy of him after all."

Liv shook her head violently. "That's BS, and you know it."

Kim wiped her tears with the back of her hand. The sooner she accepted the truth, the better now. She missed Diego as if she had a hole in her heart, but she would tailor her life better for her kids. Starting with telling Liv the truth.

"I lied to you, Liv. All those years ago when Mom left."

Liv stared at her, her gaze searching Kim's. Fear clouded her eyes. "What?"

"I found her note the previous night. She was going to take you with her."

"She didn't say a word to me."

"Because I stopped her. I threatened to tell Dad if she even touched you. I was selfish. I couldn't bear the fact that she would take you from me. I couldn't—"

"You didn't ask her why she wasn't taking *you?*"

"Everything that Dad did to you—it was my fault. If you had left with her... She *did* love you, Liv. You should know that."

Her twin laughed, the sound full of bitterness. "Isn't it weird how you're blind to what she was?" She clasped Kim's cheeks, her own eyes full of tears now. "You can't blame yourself. You did everything in your power to shield me from Dad. And Mom didn't love you *or* me— not enough. The moment you threatened her escape she decided I wasn't worth it either. Don't you see? She wasn't strong enough for that. She was never strong enough for us."

Kim's heart felt as if it was bursting with emotion. The love shining in Liv's eyes was enough to pull the last bit of wool from her eyes.

God, she had been such a fool. She had let guilt and pain rob so much from her. Her mother hadn't robbed it from her. She had done that to herself. And now she was letting her fear rob her of Diego, wasn't she? Failing herself even before she took the leap?

"And even if she had been, do you think I'd have gone with her? Left you behind?" Now her sister's words vibrated with pain. "You are my sister. You're all I had—all I *have*. What I don't get is why you have let it hurt you so much. All these years you just accepted her decision, you let it weigh everything you've done."

"What was I supposed to do?"

"You are supposed to fight for yourself. You shouldn't have let her cowardly decision have so much power over you. You always fought for me. You stood up to Dad every time he came at me. Why do you think you deserve any less?"

Kim's tears ran over her cheeks as she stared at Liv. She had no answer. It was what she was doing again with Diego. Instead of fighting for herself—fighting for her love—instead of fighting for her *babies* she was walking away to protect herself.

So what if he didn't love her? So what if he only wanted their marriage to work for the sake of the children? He took care of her, he pampered her, he understood her stubbornness and he had stood by her when she had been crumbling. It was more affection than she had ever received from anyone.

She scrubbed her cheeks and grabbed the papers from the table. "You're right. I am going to fight for myself." Her stomach churned with fear, but she couldn't let it stop her now. Her fingers shaking, she tore the documents Liv had brought into so many pieces. "Can you please call Alex? I need transportation."

Her eyes wide, Liv laughed as she followed her into her bedroom. Kim plucked at her suitcase, which she still hadn't emptied, opened it, threw the clothes into a pile and started throwing others in. Mostly shorts and tank tops, nightwear.

She slipped her laptop into its case, tucked in the power cord, followed by her cell phone charger and her wallet. She quickly called her assistant, informed her of her travel plans and hung up while the woman was still struggling to grapple with what she'd just been told.

After three years of non-stop work, Kim knew her team was obviously surprised that she was now taking vacations so frequently. But they were an expertly trained team, and she could do her job from wherever Diego was just as easily as she could in New York.

She made another call to her VP of Operations and informed her she should start a headhunt for another CEO. Effective immediately, she was going to cut down her hours. And when the time came she would need maternity leave, too.

Excitement mixed with fear thrummed through her veins, making her a little light-headed.

Liv stopped her with a hand on her shoulder. "Whoa... Kim.... Slow down." Her mobile mouth was frozen in shock. "Wow, you're really doing this."

"Yep, and I can't stop, Liv," she said, walking back into the kitchen and throwing her multivitamins into her handbag. "I have to keep moving, I have to get on a plane before I start thinking. Diego was right. I should get a device that stops my brain from overthinking."

"He said that?"

Kim nodded, the memory of his smile lending her courage.

"Alex's pilot should be ready in half an hour. Do you want me to come with you? Bring Alexander to take on Diego?"

A laugh barreled out of her and Kim kissed Liv's cheek. Hugged her again.

"No. I'm going to be fine. Whether in the name of revenge or my pregnancy, Diego always fought for us." She had to believe that and she had to do the same. "If he hadn't cared he could have sued for custody. After all the things I told him he still trusted me enough, believed in me enough, that I would love our children. He's fought for our relationship with everything he has in him. Now it's time I do the same." She clasped Liv's hands in hers, her throat closing up again. "We're good, aren't we?"

Liv nodded and kissed her cheek again. "Of course. Whatever happens, you always have me."

CHAPTER FOURTEEN

DIEGO HAD NO idea how long he had been pushing himself in the huge state-of-the-art gym that he'd had specially built on the island. His muscles groaned under the rigor he was putting himself through. It felt as if his flesh had morphed into points of torture and then turned inward.

But he couldn't stop. He hadn't been able to stop for the past week, since Kim had left. He had flown back and forth to New York within a day, worked from morning to evening and then punished himself with a brutal workout each evening, so that when he went to bed he hoped to be so exhausted that sleep came.

It hadn't worked. Even with his body turning into a bruising pulp he couldn't fall asleep. He was beginning to feel like a ticking bomb.

The days stretched torturously ahead of him, with memories of Kim pricking into him wherever he turned.

He was beginning to hate the island, after everything he had done to own it.

He'd seen Miguel and Anna poke their heads in a couple of times at the entrance to the gym.

They were worried about him. He got that. But nothing could puncture his need for physical pain right now. Nothing else could numb the emptiness he felt inside.

* * *

It was midnight by the time he walked toward his bedroom. He had showered at the gym, yelled his head off at Anna and Miguel when they'd tried to talk to him and then wandered on the beach for more than a couple of hours.

And he still wasn't tired. Every nerve in him was strung tight. Olivia would have gone to see Kim yesterday. She would have handed her his documents. He couldn't breathe for the ball of pain that was hanging around his neck.

He froze at the entrance to his bedroom.

A breeze flew in from the ocean. The French doors were wide open. The lamp was turned on, the feeble light from it illuminating the woman snoring softly in the center of his king bed.

He felt as if a tornado had hit him in the gut and then tossed him around.

How long had she been waiting for him? When had she arrived?

She was lying on her side, her knees tucked into her chest. Her arms were wrapped around herself. He didn't question why she had returned. He didn't question why she was in his bedroom, of all the rooms in the villa. They hadn't shared a bed even when she had been here.

Kim was back. The woman he loved with every breath in him was back.

He walked toward the bed, his gaze unblinking. His chest tightened and he realized the tight sensation was fear. Every inch of him was shaking with spine-chilling fear. He loved this woman so much and he was afraid to blink. He was afraid she would disappear if he did.

He climbed on to the bed slowly and pulled the cotton covers over her sleeping form.

She wore a silk sleeveless gown in dark blue that clung to the small bump at her stomach and just about covered her knees. The lace neckline fluttered over her breasts with every breeze that flew in through the door. He greedily looked over her, from her hair, which was a mess, to her painted toes.

Her long eyelashes cast shadows on her cheeks. Dark blue circles hung under her eyes. He muttered a soft curse. *Droga,* that gaunt look was back in her face again. He rubbed the pad of his thumb over her cheek, his breath hovering in his throat. And then, and only then, did he breathe air into his lungs again.

He ran his fingers over her toned arms. The skin was so soft and silky that he was afraid he would mark her with his rough fingers. His hand shaking, he pulled back.

He was never going to let her go. He had ripped out his own heart to let her go once. He couldn't do it again.

Even if he had to handcuff her to this very bed. Even if he had to spend the rest of his life tearing away her defenses piece by piece.

He didn't care anymore if she loved him or not, if she was as crazy about him as he was about her. All he wanted was to spend his life with her, looking after her, loving her, telling her every single day how much he wanted her, how much he needed her.

He stretched out next to her, feeling the weight on his shoulders dissolve into nothingness. Calm floated over him. His sore body felt lighter. He would just sit here, stay with her, watch over her.

He turned onto his side and pressed his mouth to her temple, breathed in her scent. And closed his eyes.

Sleep hit his eyelids with the force of a hurricane dragging him under, as though it hadn't eluded him at all for that whole torturous week.

Kim drifted awake suddenly, instantly registering the warm, comforting weight around her waist. It was the same feeling all over, actually. From her hair to her toes she felt as if she was encased in the most delicious embrace ever.

She opened sleep-heavy eyes. The lamp she had turned on was still lit, and Diego's sleeping face filled her vision. A soft gasp escaped her mouth. It was his arm that hung around her middle.

Her heart went from a quiet drone to a thundering pace in a mere second.

For a few minutes she just looked at him to her heart's content. He wore shorts and nothing else. She swallowed as her gaze drifted over his long, hair-roughened legs. His abdomen was a ridge of hard muscles, with a line of hair that disappeared into his shorts.

His powerfully built chest rose and fell with his even breathing. The groove where his neck met his shoulders invited her touch. She fisted her hands, her gaze on his face now.

His mouth was a lush line in repose, his features etched with the passion and kindness that made this man. How stupid had she been to walk away from him?

Taking a deep breath, she lifted the arm around her middle and twined her fingers with his long ones. She heard him breathe in on a soft hiss and froze. With a frown, she pulled his hand up and saw the raw knuckles. The skin was broken in several places and crusted with blood.

Tears hit her eyes with a brutal force. She lifted his hand to her mouth and kissed the center of his palm. She dragged her mouth over the rough calluses, learning and loving every inch of him anew.

His breathing altered from its soft rhythm to a sharp intake of breath. She froze with the tips of his fingers on her mouth.

Their gazes collided. Her fingers tightened around his. "You have to stop fighting Miguel and whoever else you are."

Warmth filtered into his gaze. "I wasn't fighting."

She fought to keep the tears at bay. "Then what is this?"

He shrugged.

"It hurts when I see you hurt, Diego. I don't ever want to see *this*," she said loudly, pointing his own fingers in his face, "again."

She couldn't keep the demand out of her tone.

She expected him to mock her, question her, tease her at least.

He said nothing, his gaze raking her face hungrily. His silent nod was too much to bear.

He scooted closer, his body an inviting fortress of pulsing heat and so much more. He still didn't say anything, didn't ask her anything. Just held her, his leg thrown over hers, his open palm on her back.

She pulled his hand to her face.

He obliged her without a word, his long fingers fanning out from her temples to her mouth. She kissed every finger, every ridge and mound of his palm.

She shivered as a sob built in her chest.

She drew a painful breath and tucked her face into his chest. She kissed him, the thundering boom of his heart the only sound filling her ears. "I've torn up the divorce papers. I never want to see them again in this lifetime. I'm never leaving you again, Diego. *Ever.*"

She felt his silent nod as he pulled her against him, his arms tight bands around her. *Why didn't he say anything?* His agonizing silence, compared to his usually mocking, challenging, probing self, was beginning to breathe crippling fear into her limbs.

Her throat was choked up with all the words she wanted to say, her strength once again leaving her in her moment of need. But she had to do this. She had to tell him, had to show him her heart.

She struggled against him and he loosened his hold.

Using his strength, she pulled herself up. She laughed, the sound tinged with her fear. She breathed hard, her hands going to her small belly. "I'm already a little clumsy."

He stayed on his side, propped by his elbow, his gaze on her belly. "You've begun to show."

She laughed, her tears finally spilling from her eyes. *He was still speaking to her. It was more than she deserved.* "Every day is making a difference."

"Can I touch you?"

"You don't have to ask," she whispered, wondering if she had already lost him. Because Diego never asked. He manipulated her, he tricked her, he bargained with her. It was the only way she had ever given him anything, the only way she had let him see anything. And his solemn request now pierced her.

He placed his hand on her belly, his huge palm almost spanning the small bump.

She placed her hand atop his and he glanced up toward her. "Aren't you going to ask me why I came back?"

The warmth disappeared from his gaze. He pulled himself up with a smooth movement and joined her against the headboard. "No."

She held his hand tightly, drawing strength from it. One question swirled on the tip of her tongue, gouging into her. Every instinct inside her told her to embrace the silence again, to let it go. If she didn't ask, she couldn't be hurt by his answer. If she didn't ask, she could...

She was short-changing herself again.

"I...I would like to ask *you* something. And I want you to give me an honest answer, okay?"

He nodded, his gaze never leaving hers.

Her throat almost seized up. There was a hot prickle of tears at the backs of her eyes. "You... Why did you take Marissa with you? I... It was the cruelest thing you could

have done to me. I knew Eduardo. I would have come with
you…"

He touched his mouth to her temple. "Shh…I never
meant to hurt you."

His fingers tightened around hers. He didn't smile, but
she saw the softening in his eyes. Because he understood
how big it was for her just to ask.

"I wanted to take you with me. All I wanted was to hear
you say again and again that you weren't disgusted by what
I had done, that I was a better man than I already was." His
words were soft, yet loaded with emotion. "But, Eduardo,
he was always a good reminder to me of what I could become if I let something matter to me too much. Leaving
without you was a matter of denying myself, proving to myself that I didn't need you. Marissa…when she requested if
she could come I couldn't say no."

"I want to share both good and bad with you, Diego. I
want to be the one you lean on when…" She took a deep
breath. "I meant what I said before. I'm never leaving
again."

A fire licked into life in his gaze. "That's good to know."

"Why are you being like this?"

"What is it you want from me? I will do it."

"You have given up on me."

Fresh tears spilled from her eyes, but she wiped them
with determination. This was only one day—the beginning.
She would spend this entire lifetime and more waiting for
his love. Because this man—he meant everything to her.
And she wasn't going to hide how she felt for him either.

"I'm in love with you, Diego." She rushed over words
that should be said slowly, softly, without waiting for his
reaction. She could do this only one way. "I've always been
in love with you. I was an idiot before. I'm going to spend
the rest of my life fighting for us, proving to you that I'm
worth it. All I ask is—"

In a second he was kneeling over her, his legs on either side of hers. And then he kissed her. She moaned and wrapped her hands around his nape. Gave his kiss everything she had in her. He wasn't gentle with her. His hand in her hair kept her where he wanted her as his tongue plunged into her mouth.

Heat blasted all over her as he pushed up her nightgown with rough hands. His hands cupped her breasts and she whimpered at the pleasure sparking all over.

"Diego, wait…" she managed to say, even as arousal stole through her, lighting an insatiable fire in her body.

He halted, his breathing rough, his palms spread out over her thighs. His face was tight with guilt. "Did I hurt you?"

She laughed and cupped his jaw, her breathing still nowhere near normal. "I won't break, Diego. I want nothing more than to feel you inside me." Stealing her fingers into his hair, she pressed an open-mouthed kiss to his lips. Warmth stole through her. Diego's groan added to it. "But I… You haven't said anything. I understand if you're angry, if you're—"

"Angry?" he said, and the very emotion he was denying crept into his tone. "Try gut-twisting emptiness. I've never been more alone, felt more alone in my life than the past week. Everything I have achieved, everything I have—it means nothing without you."

Her heart leaped into her throat. She felt dizzy—as though someone had sucked out the oxygen from around them.

He touched his forehead to hers. "I love you so much, *minha esposinha.*" His words reverberated with pain. His features were stark and menacing. "And if you leave me again it will destroy the little good there is in me. It almost did this time."

Her heart felt as if it would burst out of her chest. Kim wrapped her arms around him and hugged him so tight that her breathing stuttered. It was more than she had ever hoped for. "You love me?"

His gaze was filled with pain. "I can survive if I lose all this wealth, I have survived rejection from pretty much everyone in my life, but I can't survive losing you. When you left, for a few moments all I could think was that you had gone because everything I had done wasn't enough. *I* wasn't enough."

"No, Diego. Don't say that. You're the most wonderful man I've ever met. I just couldn't bear to be by your side thinking that you would never love me. It hurt so much that you turned away from me. I wanted to ask you. I wanted to…" She shivered and he kissed her temple. "It was nothing to do with you, Diego. I was weak. I…"

"You're stubborn, arrogant, you drive me to the worst of myself and you're so damn hard to get through to sometimes. But you're the toughest woman I know and I love you for everything you are."

He settled his palm on her belly and she wondered if she would combust from the pride, from the acceptance, from the love in his words.

"I can't think of a better, stronger mother for my children."

This fierce, passionate man loved her. She would count herself lucky for the rest of her days. "You really think that, don't you? I couldn't believe you trusted me enough to…"

"Of course I do. You might not feel that connection, but I have no doubt that you'll love our children."

Kim smiled and hid her face in the crook of his elbow, his words washing over her with a warmth she wanted to keep close. She would tell him in a minute. She would tell him how much joy now flew through her just at the thought of their little family.

"Will you promise me you will never stop fighting for

me and you will never give up on me? Even when I don't believe I'm worthy of you?" she said, fear stealing through her.

He met her gaze and smiled, his hands tight against her waist. And the tenderness in it stole through her. "We will always fight for each other. We will never let ourselves settle for anything less than we deserve. It's a promise, *gatinha*."

Olivia laughed as strong arms engulfed her from behind and pulled her hard into a body she would know in her sleep. She clamped Alexander's arms with her fingers, tucking herself even tighter into his embrace.

She should have known he would follow her to Diego's island.

"You left without telling me," he whispered near her ear, his hands holding her hard at her ribcage.

Liv closed her eyes and breathed the essence of him, every inch of her trembling with that same happiness that had marked her life the past couple of months.

"I was worried about her," she said, nodding toward Kim.

Kim and Diego were walking hand in hand at the edge of the water on the beach, lost in each other. Liv couldn't stop smiling at how Diego's hand never left her twin, how Kim hadn't stopped smiling ever since Liv had gotten here.

Alexander kissed her jaw, his hands inching under her T-shirt until they found bare skin. She sucked in a breath at the weight of his palm.

"There's no need, is there?" he asked.

"No need," Liv repeated, knowing that he understood. "He loves her, Alexander. Like she deserves to be loved." She swallowed the tears in her throat. This was a time to rejoice. "I've never seen her so happy and glowing. And did you know she's having—?"

He turned her around, his blue gaze eating her up with

a hungry intensity that started an ache in her own body. It was always like that.

But he looked haunted, with deep grooves pinching his mouth. "You got on a plane without telling me after we had a God-awful fight, Liv. You weren't answering your phone. I asked Emily. She thought it was really funny that I didn't know where my wife was before she told me. I think my heart stopped for a few moments."

The edge in his words, the way he was holding her so tight… Liv frowned. Damn her and her impulsive head. "I left my phone by accident. And I should have realized Emily would play with you first. I *was* really worried about Kim. And I'm sorry about Emily. I know I shouldn't interfere, but—"

He pressed a soft kiss to her mouth, his hands capturing her face. The love that shone in his gaze took her breath away. "I think I know why you did that. It's a strange feeling to be protected by my ferocious wife. I love you, Liv," he whispered.

God, she would never tire of hearing him say it.

"And I'm glad Kim has found happiness."

Liv nodded and returned his kiss, her own joy making her light-headed. She twined her fingers with his and tugged him forward. "It's time you met Diego properly, don't you think?"

She laughed when he raised his brows in an exaggerated way. Her husband and her twin's husband were just as different as she and Kim were.

Life was going to be really interesting for them, but full of laughter and love.

* * * * *